Lucidity

An Aja Holland Novel

Willow River Press is an imprint of Between the Lines Publishing. The Willow River Press name and logo are trademarks of Between the Lines Publishing.

Between the Lines Publishing
1769 Lexington Ave N, Ste 286
Roseville MN 55108
btwnthelines.com

First Published: May 2023

ISBN: (Paperback) 978-1-958901-54-0

ISBN: (Ebook) 978-1-958901-55-7

Lucidity

An Aja Holland Novel

the way the day begins decides the shade of everything

but the way it ends depends on if you're home

"New York Morning"

Elbow

Morning

Chapter One

Pavlov would undoubtedly agree there is no conditioned response stronger than a response conditioned by thirty years of routine. That Jocko Morahan even bothered to set his alarm at night was a conditioned act in itself since, in another conditioned act, he regularly and invariably awoke a few minutes before it went off at 4:45 the following morning. Even before his eyes had begun to creep open, he was reaching out to his nightstand where he knew he'd find the ancient Westclox to stifle the alarm. Whether this was about avoiding the grating clang of the alarm or avoiding the pissing and moaning said clanging would bring from the figure on the other side of the bed, fetally curled into a tight round ball under the covers, remained an eternal open question, even in his own mind.

Morahan lay there for a bit, nothing on his mind other than how to slide, pull, and writhe his stiff body out of the bed without stirring the bed's other occupant. Of late, he'd noticed how much more difficult this was becoming. Joints bent only stiffly, often made little popping noises, and, he thought, grimly, there must've been a time when he'd been able to do this without so much grunting.

Despite all the grunting and popping and even a little moaning, he got to his feet, flinching at the cold floor able to bite through the threadbare rug. The glowing space heater in a corner of the small bedroom didn't seem to be doing much against the pre-dawn chill. Either that, he thought ruefully, or – like everything else -- the pre-dawn chill was getting to him in a way it hadn't used to.

He walked as lightly as his round, little form could, trying not to tease noises up from the warped-wood floor which seemed to have its own reasons for moaning. All that ginger moving, and easy stepping disintegrated once his feet hit the cold tiles of the bathroom.

"JesusMotherMaryChrist!" It came out in a streaming hiss. He looked behind him to make sure he hadn't awakened the balled-up figure in bed.

Another of Morahan's perennial questions to himself: Does she really sleep through this? Or is the old cow an Academy Award-worthy fake?

Jocko and Violet Morahan lived in a small four room apartment above "Morahan's" – a combination convenience store, coffee shop, saloon, and gas station on what passed for Warsaw's main drag; a two-lane stretch of Route 201, what the old timers sometimes called the Old Canada Road when they wanted to sound like old timers. Morahan came down the narrow, creaking steps which led into the cramped kitchen behind the dining room. He flicked on the room lights and then the outside signs for "Food," "Fuel," "Drinks," "Morahan's," then unlocked the front door.

He pulled on his ragged-edged cammo hunting jacket and steeled himself before stepping outside, but his steeling abilities were fading these days along with his joint flexibility. The October morning chill drilled deep into his bones to stir more aches and set him shivering. Still, things needed doing and he headed for the gas pumps to open the service ports and check if the paper rolls in the receipt dispensers needed changing. He doubted it; there were days he could count on both hands the vehicles passing by; most of them lumber haulers heading south for the paper mill down Skowhegan, the closer Madison mill having closed some years ago. There were times he could go weeks without having to replace the roll.

"Mr. Twombley?" The voice was feeble, quivering, Morahan almost hadn't heard it, what with his own shivering. "Mr. Twombley!"

Morahan turned. The sun hadn't cleared the horizon yet, the air was still grey and blue, everything more shadow than substance. It took him a second, trying to focus for distance through his bifocals to see one of those shadows on the road, a vaguely human shape maybe fifteen yards or so distant, hanging on to the bullet-holed "Moose Crossing" sign on the road shoulder.

The sun must have crept up another degree at that moment, because everything began to seem a shade less gray, a shade more substantial. The figure was a man, eyebrow-raisingly out of place in a sport jacket and tie, now stumbling and wavering his way along the shoulder toward Morahan.

"Mr. Twombley, help me!" the man called out – more of a gasp, a last gasp as it turned out. The man took a final step, then dropped to his knees as he reached out toward Morahan who remained frozen at the gas pumps, still trying to make sense of what he was seeing and, even more so, hearing. Then the man fell forward onto the wet grass and lay there, still.

Jocko Morahan blinked once, twice, looked up and down the empty highway. The handful of tired-looking houses scattered along the roadside were still dark, and so was the sagging clapboard used-to-be church where Crazy Carl, who kept all sorts of odd hours working on Warsaw's cars and appliances and whatever, lived, and old Cargill, whose work hours seemed wholly dependent on his mood, had yet to open his general store. The fields across the road and, beyond them, the band of the Kennebec River, were lost in the morning gloom but were quiet and still, even the river it seemed. It only slowly came to Morahan that whatever was going to be done about this had to be done by him.

"Oh, crap," and he ran as fast as his stubby, stiff legs would allow, toward the man lying in the road.

Chapter Two

"Doc?"

Liz Tilley came to just enough consciousness to feel a light, tentative touch on her shoulder, barely shaking her. It was light enough that she could dismiss it as a half-dream/half-memory: being gently rocked awake by her dad for school, not so gently shaken awake by a panicky, confused intern while she tried to catch a few z's in a Mass General doctor's lounge. Whatever; it wasn't real, so she curled herself a little more tightly, more warmly under her three comforters, and started to let herself slip back -- .

"Doc!"

Ok, that was real. She cracked one eye open ever so slightly, until she saw the worry-furrowed face of Jocko Morahan hanging over her.

"Jesus, Christ, Jocko!" And now she was awake, making sure nothing embarrassing might be peeking out from under the comforters.

"Hate to wake you, Doc — "

"I hate you waking me."

"It's an emergency, Doc."

"Always. Where?"

"My place."

"A few minutes," and she shooed Morahan out with a tired wave of her hand.

She didn't move for a bit, partly because she was still waking up, partly dwelling on the not completely unpleasant thought that, *This is what you signed up for, Lady: a place with no locks on the doors, where everybody thinks they're your pal, personal privacy is an alien concept, and your time belongs to everybody who knows you.*

Whatever shreds of sleep Liz was still holding on to evaporated immediately once she stepped out of her house and the cold morning air hit her. She pulled her plaid flannel coat a little tighter around her, or as well as she could with one cold hand pulled up inside a sleeve, and the other one similarly trying to stay warm with just one exposed finger looped around the handle of her medical bag. She clomped/shuffled across the road in her bulky, untied Carhartts boots to Morahan's place. Even from the apron around the fuel pumps, she could see through the store's plate glass front window at what she'd probably been called for.

There was a man sitting at one of the tables, holding a bloody bar towel to his forehead. He was maybe a little older than her, close to forty she guessed, and couldn't have looked more out of place in Warsaw than if he'd been part of a delegation from Mars: tweed sport coat, tie, corduroy slacks. She paused to take a quick look around, look for a car, crashed Lear jet, or alien spacecraft to account for the man's presence, then went into Morahan's.

She nodded at the man who didn't look up, didn't seem to notice her at all. She heard Morahan clattering around in the kitchen, no doubt prepping for the few heads he referred to, without the slightest facetiousness, as "the breakfast crowd."

"Jocko!"

"Yo!"

"Coffee!" Then, after another look at the man, "Make it two! And some ice!"

She pulled up a chair to sit in front of the man, offered the requisite routine comforting smile and beckoned him to remove the towel. Without looking up, he let his hand with the towel drop, revealing an ugly gash across half his forehead.

"Ouch," she said.

"I agree," the man grumbled.

She reached into her bag, pulled on a pair of surgical gloves.

"You're a doctor?"

"Some think so," she said.

Close up, she could get a better look at him. A square, serious but not unpleasant face, maybe a little younger than she'd first thought but worn in an undefinable way. Something -- not age or whatever had put that ding in his forehead – was taking a toll in his face, in those gray eyes. There was an overnight's growth of whiskers, a full head of dark hair with light touches of gray around the temples that, despite its morning-after muss, she could tell was cut with the kind of finesse you didn't get at a neighborhood barber shop (not that Warsaw had one). His clothes were mottled with damp spots, soaked through, as if he'd been laying in the dewy grass for some time. His expensive-looking ox blood oxfords were caked with still-damp mud.

Morahan was back with two mugs of steaming black coffee and a small saucer of ice cubes.

The man squinted up at Morahan. "You brought me here?"

"You don't 'member?"

"I'm a little…" and he faded out, but his eyes went past Morahan. Liz followed the man's gaze to the two over/under shotguns mounted crosswise over the bar.

Liz took one of the cubes and ran it gently along the swollen tissue on either side of the wound and that unsurprisingly brought his attention back to her.

"Ow."

"Sorry," she said. "I'm trying to get the swelling down."

"Are you a doctor?"

"You already asked me that."

"Oh, man…" He seemed daunted by his own fogginess. "I hope you said yes."

"You can hope."

"Where am I?"

"Bleedin' on my damn floor is where," Morahan said with a glum look at the rust-colored blotches on the linoleum. He picked up the stained dish towel. "Never gettin' that out."

"What happened?" Liz asked the man.

"Hm?" The man appeared to have drifted off.

"What-happened-to-you?"

"I think…I think there was a car accident."

"You think?"

"I'm…not…" He shook his head.

Liz started cleaning the wound with disinfectant. The man winced. "Yeah, I know," she said, wincing sympathetically. "Jocko, I think you better get Alfie."

Morahan was still looking mournfully at his wasted bar towel. "Ya know what these things cost? I gotta go down Lewiston, all that way, restaurant supply place."

"Jocko: Alfie!"

"He's probably still asleep."

Liz took a patient breath. "Then I suggest you wake his ass up."

"He gets cranky when you wake him up."

"Didn't stop you waking *me* up!"

Morahan grabbed his cammo jacket. "Keep an eye on the place, eh, Doc?" as he headed out.

"Yeah, I'll try to keep the throngs at bay."

The man's groggy eyes cleared a bit, not in a good way, when Liz brought a syringe out of her medical bag. "Um…"

"I'm going to give you some Lidocaine, numb you up there. You need stitches and that won't tickle otherwise. The needle's going to sting a bit."

The man's face puckered with the first prick of the needle. "It did. I don't know if I asked this already; where am I?"

"Besides bleeding on Jocko Morahan's floor? Warsaw."

"I'm assuming not the one in Poland."

"Warsaw, Maine."

The man's eyes widened, again. "I'm in *Maine*?"

"Where'd you think you were?"

"I -- …" His face went blank. "I don't know." He frowned as he watched her take tissue forceps, needle holder, and suture from her bag.

"Don't worry," Liz said. "I'm a skilled professional." She held the needle holder up to him.

"Don't get nervous, but do you know what this thingie is for?"

"Excuse me?"

"Kidding. Relax. Sadly, I get so much practice doing this kind of thing around here, I could do this with my eyes closed. Want to see?"

"Madam, you've got a hell of a sense of humor."

"Up here, one has to have one."

He turned again, to look at the shotguns over the bar.

"What is it?" she asked.

"I was, um, wondering... Are those just for show?"

"Oh, no, Jocko uses them. Don't worry. He hardly ever uses them on customers. Hardly."

He mustered a weak grin. "More jokes?"

"You better hope I'm joking. He likes to show them off since they're the only thing he owns worth a damn."

The man turned back to the shotguns, his head cocked; Liz could see he was reaching for something but couldn't quite grasp it. Finally, with a shake of his head, he let it go.

By the time Morahan returned with Alfie Aubry in tow, Liz had stitched about half of the man's wound closed.

"Did I miss any customers?" Morahan asked anxiously.

"You're kidding, right?" Liz said.

Aubry gently pushed Morahan aside and stepped up.

Liz had long ago noted that Warsaw, like the rest of rural Maine, was, bit by bit, turning into a repository for the middle-aged and aging. Kid got old enough for a driver's license and he/she was gone: off to college, off hunting for a job, off looking for…something, *anything*. Alfie Aubry, like much of the population of Warsaw, was pushing fifty. Still, Liz thought, he was an amazing specimen in that no matter how much nutritionless junk he stuffed in himself from Jocko Morahan's stock, he remained a tall, almost skeletal figure, with a full head of salt-and-pepper hair that rarely saw a comb. His leathery face was as rumpled as the often food/drink-stained and ill-fitting uniform – sleeves too short for his gangly arms, too-big pants bunched by a belt at his narrow waist -- Liz could never remember seeing ironed.

Aubry had a tendency to slouch, as if his spindly frame couldn't adequately support the weight of his top end with its massive push broom mustache, but now he cleared his throat and drew himself up to his considerable height. "This him?" he asked no one in particular, trying to sound authoritative and not doing a very good job of it.

Liz turned to give him an are-you-serious look.

Aubry shrugged: ok, not the best way to start. "Jocko here, Mr. Morahan, I mean, he says you come walkin' down the road, said somethin' 'bout a car accident?"

"If that's what he says…"

Aubry shook his head, confused by the response.

"Thing is," the man sighed, "I don't remember."

"You don't 'member comin' up the road, seein' Mr. Morahan here."

"Nope."

"He's suffered quite a knock to the noggin, Alfie," Liz said. "He's probably concussed."

"Who're you?" the man asked Aubry.

"Constable Aubry."

The man looked questioningly to Liz. "Constable?"

"Translation," Liz said, "small town cop."

"He's it?"

Liz nodded. "All of it."

The man didn't say it out loud, but his face flashed a resigned, Oh-oh.

Aubry took a moment to consider his next move, his thumb and index finger ruffling his mustache, then rustled around in one of his duty jacket's pockets and came out with a small notebook. He kept patting his pockets, looking for something. "Um," was all he had to say with a pained look to Morahan who rolled his eyes as he went over to the bar and brought back a pencil. "How 'bout a coffee, Jocko, 'n' maybe grab me a pack a those Swiss rolls on the way back."

Morahan headed for the kitchen, grumbling a concern about who was paying for all this coffee largesse.

Aubry flicked the notebook open, shifted on his feet as if he was preparing for some great endeavor, poised his pencil over the first blank page. "Let's get your name."

"My name?"

"Seems a good place to start."

Liz watched the man's mouth open, then freeze, his pale grey eyes rapidly shift from surprise to confusion to…panic. "I…I don't know." What that actually meant seemed to dawn on him slowly, and then, *I don't know!* His chest started pumping up and down, a frantic bellows.

"Relax," Liz said. She snipped off the tail end of the suture and began applying gauze over the wound. "I said that was a hell of a knock you took. You're going to be fuzzy for a while."

"Let's make it easy," Aubry said. "Why'nt you show me your ID?"

The man started patting at his pockets. "ID?"

"Lemme see your wallet."

"I, uh, I don't seem to have, um…" Again, that same panicked look.

"Ok, let's try this," Aubry said, and Liz could see he was bouncing between frustration, thinking he might be getting jerked around, and pure puzzlement. "Empty your pockets. Put everything on the table."

The man stood too quickly and immediately began wavering on his feet. Liz reached out to steady him.

"Are you hurt anywhere else?" she asked.

"Feels like *everywhere* else."

"Does sound like a car accident," Liz said to Aubry.

The man went through one pocket after another but the only thing that wound up on the table was a book of matches; black cover, with "Champagne" written in hot pink script across the image of crossed champagne flutes.

"That it?" Aubry asked.

The man nodded.

"Were you robbed?"

The man's mouth worked but managed only something like a resigned sigh combined with a cross between a shrug and shake of his head. He dropped heavily back into his chair.

Liz took the man's wrists in her hands. He let her. She held his right wrist up to Alfie, showing him a band of pale skin. "Maybe that answers your question." She also noted – with a slight mental reprimand that she'd even thought to look -- there was no such band on his left ring finger.

"Do you normally wear a watch?" Aubry asked but the man could only do that helpless shrug/nod thing again.

"I wouldn't push him too hard, Alfie," Liz cautioned. "Like I keep telling you: he took a hell of a conk."

"So's you keep sayin'."

There was a screech of tires on macadam, and Liz couldn't help but notice the comic effect of their three heads – hers, Aubry's, the man's, turning in unison toward the front window. Even Morahan stuck his head out of the kitchen at the noise.

Headlights swept through the dining room as a car on the highway reversed, revved enough to bring a chirp from its spinning tires, before its nose whipped around and the car vaulted onto the pump apron, heading for Morahan's so fast, Liz wondered – and flinched along with the others – if it'd stop in time. The car lurched to a violent halt, the driver's door popped open and a young fellow, looking as out of place as the injured man in designer jeans, brilliantly white Reeboks, and a GQ-caliber frock-length leather jacket, jumped out and ran for the door.

He froze at the door, taking in the frozen, fixed-eyed quartet inside, looked at first surprised at Aubry then smiled in relief before coming in.

"Jesus, I'm glad to see you guys!" he gasped. "I was trying to call 911, but nothing, I got nothing -- "

"Dead zone," Aubry said. "We're in a dead zone."

"Yeah, right, I figured," the adrenaline-fueled words tumbled over each other, "I was looking for, ya know, a phone, I was going so fast I almost passed this place, ran right by it, but I saw the lights, the lights, then I saw *you* –" and he pointed to Aubry, " – thank *God*, because a cop, well, that's why I was trying to call 911 -- "

"Whoa whoa whoa, slow down a bit," Aubry said. "Why'd you need a policeman?"

The newcomer pointed off down the road. "An accident, I guess, looks like an accident, a car, looks like a car went off the road, maybe a mile that way."

At that, all heads now turned to the injured man.

The newcomer pointed at him. "That your car?"

"Well, that's a question," Aubry said, frowning down at the injured man, "Ain't it?"

For the first time, Liz saw the fog in the injured man's eyes clear, and it was a pained, alarmed clarity. "What about the woman? Is she ok?"

Now it was the newcomer's turn to look lost. "What woman?"

Chapter Three

"Could you crank up the heat a bit, Alfie?"

"It *is* up. 'S good's it's gonna get. Been meanin' to have Carl take a look at it," which didn't stop Aubry from fiddling with the heater controls.

Liz and the injured man were crammed into the back seat of Aubry's ancient Jeep Wrangler, a vehicle so spotted with rust and primer cover-ups the local joke was it was some kind of camouflage pattern. Liz had found an oil-spotted blanket jammed under the seat and thrown it over the man's shoulders, but he was still shivering.

"That's it! Right there!" This was the new guy, bouncing excitedly in his seat and almost taking Aubry's eye out as he pointed to the boxy vehicle ahead on the opposite side of the road, nose down on the embankment, front end buried in the high grass, passenger door hanging wide open. They were about a mile south of Warsaw.

Aubry pulled the Wrangler over onto the near shoulder, sat for a long moment, engine idling, studying the car. The sun still hadn't broken the horizon, but the open fields of high grass and shrubs beyond the off-roaded car were changing from pre-dawn grayness to dew-glistening green under a thin layer of breeze-rippling mist.

After a bit, Aubry gave a long, meditative sigh, but Liz knew that was typical of him. It was easy to think of Aubry as dim on first meeting him, but she'd been in Warsaw long enough to know that he was someone who liked to take his time thinking through his moves before he made them.

He pulled out his notebook, made some notes as he studied the car. "You come here in a time machine?" he finally asked the injured man.

"Hm?"

"What is that? It's older than this wreck."

"Ford Bronco. Nineteen-ninety."

Aubry slowly turned to the man, his bushy eyebrows slowly raising. "So that *is* your vehicle? You seem to know it pretty good."

But the man made some kind of face, not quite a frown. Liz got the impression he was again mentally reaching for something…but couldn't quite grasp it.

"Well?" Aubry pushed. "Is it?"

"Yeeeaaah…"

"But?"

The man still couldn't get hold of it. "Something else." But then just looked helplessly at Aubry.

By now, Aubry – like Liz – had come to expect this kind of thing from the man. "Riiiight," Aubry said with a sighed resignation. "Well, you kept it in better shape than mine." Low bar though that might be, Liz thought the Bronco looked shockingly pristine, same as it had when it rolled off the showroom floor.

Aubry turned to the new guy. "Your name?"

"Gilbert Parfitt. People call me Gilly. I hate Gilbert."

"I can understand that," Aubry said, making the note, "though I'm not sure 'Gilly' 's a whole lot better." Aubry finally killed the engine, did another of those contemplative fingertip run-throughs of his mustache, then opened his door. "You wanna get out, fine, but stay around my Jeep. Don't want nobody clompin' 'round down there just yet."

Liz smiled; slow talking, slow moving, but never underestimate the man.

As Aubry walked toward the Bronco, giving it a wide berth while he checked out the ground, Parfitt climbed out, then Liz and the injured man. She had to help him: his various aches and pains didn't make climbing out of the Wrangler easy, and as soon as he got to his feet on the road he began to waver until Liz propped him up against the side of the Jeep. His shivering grew worse.

"Why don't you get back in the Jeep?"

"It's not any warmer in there."

She had to grin at that because he was right. She started to strip off her coat. "Take this."

"I couldn't – "

"I'm layered up, I'll be fine." She wasn't just being nice. When she had first moved up to Warsaw, the locals had told her there'd be fall days where the temperature could vary 15-20 degrees between morning and nightfall. "Layer up," they told her. "Strip down as it gets warmer, put 'em back on when it gets colder." So, on these chill mornings, her standard attire was a cami, thermal top, New England Patriots jersey, a flannel long sleeve, then her flannel coat. "At least let me -- ..." And she draped her jacket over the blanket around his shoulders.

Liz watched Aubry circle the Bronco slowly, finally stopping at a place a few feet from the open passenger door. He waved the three of them over, held up a hand to stop them at the shoulder, looking down the embankment. He pointed to a depression in the shin-high grass. "Looks like this is where you were layin'. A while, I'd guess, to make that kind of impression. I don't suppose you 'member when all this happened?" Familiar helpless shrug from the injured man, same resigned sigh from Aubry. "I didn't think so."

Aubry turned back to the Bronco and slid inside. Liz could see him rooting around in the glove compartment

– "No registration, no insurance card" -- then leaning over toward the driver's side, fiddling with something, heard a metallic click. "Musta been a while ago; she won't start, battery's dead. Looks like the lights were on all night. Hey, Doc, I need you to look at this."

Parfitt offered to replace Liz as someone the injured man could lean on. Aubry slid back out of the Bronco to make room for Liz. He pointed to a rust-colored splotch on the Bronco's dash in front of the passenger seat.

"That look like blood to you, Doc?"

"It does."

"Can you tell how long it's been there?"

Liz touched it lightly with a fingertip; still tacky. "Hard to tell with this temperature, the air's got a lot of moisture in it. Easily a couple of hours, I'd say, maybe more."

"That'd be about the right place for where he hit his head?"

"Just about."

"Whaddaya think about that?" and he pointed to the driver's side.

"Well, my my!" On the driver's side, there was blood pooled on the seat, where it would've collected if it had been running down someone's side. "So it does look like the guy was right; somebody else was in here with him."

Aubry walked around to the driver's door, opened it using a kerchief that looked like it had been in his back pocket for years. "Somebody bleedin' like this, could they have gone far?"

Liz shook her head. "If they were still alive when they went off the road, I wouldn't think so."

"So this couldn't be our guy's blood."

"Even if he could bleed that much and still be kicking, I don't see how blood from his head could wind up over there."

Aubry checked out the ground outside the driver's door. "I don't see no blood trail out here. You think, uh -- " and he nodded toward the injured man leaning against Parfitt " -- coulda drug her off somewheres?"

"Guy can barely hold himself up, Alfie. I'm gonna get my bag, take some blood samples just to make sure we're looking at two people."

Aubry nodded approvingly. "You! Gillhooley!"

"Gilly!"

"Whatever. You didn't see nobody else 'round here?"

"I saw the blood, so I looked, but nothing."

"Well, Alfie," Liz said as she pulled herself out of the Bronco, "looks like you're finally going to earn your meager constable's pay."

"How's that, Doc?"

"Seems like you've got an honest-to-God *Murder, She Wrote* mystery on your hands."

Chapter Four

Violet Morahan looked down at the cold tea pot on the kitchen range with the kind of disappointment that comes from having no reason to expect better yet still hoping for better, then not getting it.

"Would it kill you, just once, have me my tea water?"

Jocko didn't answer. He was busy in what he referred to, with his usual penchant for overstatement, as his "office" which was no more than a small desk jammed into the cubby under the kitchen stairs. He was rifling through the scads of paper – invoices, utility bills, old check books and the like – shoved into the desk's few cramped drawers.

"Did you hear me?"

"Busy, Vi!"

"I mean, just *once!* Surprise me! Do it and the shock'll kill me, and you won't have to worry 'bout it no more."

"*Busy!* There's coffee, have coffee."

She filled the teapot at the kitchen sink, set it on the stove, an old thing, the kind where she had to risk self-immolation as she lit the pilot light from a box of wood matches. "Thirty-three years I hate coffee, he says have coffee."

"Thirty-three years you're the only human bean don't like coffee in the morning. Do you know where the paper on this place is?"

"What paper?"

"From when we bought this place. The deed, the transfer of the liquor license, all that stuff."

"How the hell do I know? That's all your stuff in there, you know I don't go pokin' 'round in your stuff. Maybe if you kept all that crap in some kinda, you know, *order* – "

"*Not now, Vi!*" He was on his hands and knees now. One of the drawers was stuck halfway out, wedged by something which had evidently spilled out onto the rails. Jocko reached in – "C'mere, ya sonofa – *Gotcha!*" He pulled himself back into his chair, unfurling the crumpled document. He looked up, saw Violet hovering over the stove in her wooly robe, flannel p.j.s,, furry slippers and a sleep cap puffed up by her curlered hair. "Jesus, Violet, this what you want customers to see?"

If body language could be sarcastic, then the way Violet made a show of shuffling to the kitchen doorway, carefully studying the empty dining room, then shuffling back to the stove was positively acerbic. "Well, my love, I don't see the problem."

From the Wrangler's back seat, Liz could see Aubry slowly tilting his head from one side to the other, like he was trying to get things in his head to fall into some kind of order. "Listen here, Mr. Profit – "

"Parfitt, but, like I said, you can call me Gilly," which, from what Liz could see in the rearview mirror, Aubry seemed to favor like a piece of meat gone bad.

"Whatever," Aubry said, stroking his mustache with his free hand. "See, here it is, sun's not even up yet, and here you are, and Warsaw, bless it, ain't all that close to anything. So's the question I got is -- "

"What am I doing here?"

"Kinda hit it on the head there."

Parfitt shook his head, gave a wryly amused, "Huh." "Same question I'm asking myself."

"Sorry?"

"Ok, that didn't come out right. Thing is, I'm a journalist. Kind of. Well, not really."

Poor Aubry's head went from that slow side-to-side to a dazed shake. "Do you not know what you do for a livin'?"

Parfitt shifted uncomfortably in his seat; a man embarrassed. "See, thing is, I write for one of those weeklies the housewives buy at the supermarket. You know: how to lose weight, recipes, knit your own placemats, that kind of stuff. I feel kind of like a pompous ass calling myself a journalist, writing that kind of goo."

Aubry shrugged. "Not judging, young fella. Still seems a bit early to be on the road 'n' it don't tell me what you're doin' way up here."

"We're based in Portland, I'm heading to Canada, I'm supposed to meet somebody to tour me around this afternoon. They've got me on this piece: 'The Delectables of Rural Quebec'."

"What delectables?"

Parfitt shrugged. "I'll find out when I get there."

Instead of pulling into Morahan's, Aubry rolled on a little further and pulled into the muddy drive leading up a low knoll to the church where Crazy Carl lived. "You folks don't mind, I got to arrange to get that car brought in. You can walk over to Jocko's if you want, but I won't be long."

The church was a very New Englandy clapboard affair, but the white paint was pealing in some places, flaked off in others, and generally weathered into a dull gray. Out front was a makeshift, slightly off-kilter flagpole made from a stripped pine trunk flying a faded and frayed American flag, and a faded and frayed black POW/MIA flag. They drove up past the flagpole and Aubry rolled to a stop.

"I want to get out," the injured man said. "I feel like the more I'm on my feet, the better I'm going to feel."

"Not the soundest medical advice," Liz said, "but suit yourself. You're in for something of an adventure in Wonderland."

She let that puzzle the man as they clambered out, following Aubry around to the back of the church where they could hear metallic clanging interrupted by the high-pitched whine of some kind of power tool. The working noises were barely perceptible through the blaring music; tinny and distorted and *loud*; Billy Corgan screeching through the chorus of Smashing Pumpkins' "Cherub Rock" –

Let meeee ouuuuuut

Let meee ouuuuut…

That seemed to be enough to have Parfitt elect to stay in the Jeep.

The open ground around the church – maybe a quarter-acre or so -- was littered with all sorts of household appliances – washing machines and dryers, refrigerators, freezers, stoves, soft drink machines, espresso machines…if it belonged in a kitchen or even fit on a countertop, it was out there. And then there were cars, pick-up trucks, campers, some looking pretty recent, some resting on tire-less wheels looking as if they'd been sitting out there since the long-ago year they came off the production line. And there was furniture:

dressers, dining tables, an assortment of pieces to sit on from dining room chairs to cushioned love seats, all in some state of disrepair; from mild to what's-still-holding-it-together. But there seemed a (barely) perceptible order to it all, separated by category and within each category, the obviously derelict from the salvageable.

There was a workspace close by the church made of patio brick, so defined by the sawhorses, tool-littered work bench, and the hulk of a man bent over and elbow deep in the guts of an upended Frigidaire which looked to date back to poodle skirts and saddle shoes. Badly mounted on another makeshift tree mast, overhanging the workspace, was a gratingly tinny loudspeaker, its dented bell looking like it had been worked over with a ball peen hammer.

The man working on the fridge had his back to them until Aubry quietly said – as quietly as he could and still be heard over Corgan's guttural growls -- "Hey, Carl," in a way indicating one didn't make loud noises around Carl, and Liz had lived in Warsaw long enough to know that you didn't.

Carl froze for a second, as if processing the sound, then his broad shoulders relaxed, he eased up out of the fridge and turned. From the day she'd met him, Liz always thought of Carl as what a middle-aged Viking would look like; a beer-and-burger gut, but still with broad, squared shoulders, Popeye forearms, and thick-fingered hands that when clenched looked like the heads of ten-pound sledges. His gray, squiggly hair was pulled back in a ponytail running down to his shoulder blades, and his broad, weather-beaten face was framed by a tangled salt-and-pepper beard matching his equally tangled salt-and-pepper brows. Visible through his open down vest, stretched across his wide chest and the bulge of his belly was a faded black T-shirt adorned with the age-cracked silk-screen image of the Grateful Dead's *Blues for Allah* fiddle-playing skeleton. Sticking out from all that facial brush, the breeze across the top of the knoll enveloping them all in its heady fragrance, was a half-smoked Cheech & Chong-sized joint.

Liz turned to give the stranger with the dented head a "He's safe" smile but saw he wasn't quite buying the message, blinking disbelievingly like he was wondering if this was some manifestation of his head wound.

"What say, Carl?" Aubry asked.

Suddenly, that fleshy face which had been folded in a suspicious frown, unfurled into a smile of fearfully massive teeth. He took the joint out of his mouth, dabbed it out on his tongue before pocketing it. "Alfie! *Alfie!*" It was a gravelly baritone bellow. "My man! My *man!*" He scooped Aubry up in his thick arms in a rib-crushing hug that lifted the constable off his feet, before he dropped him back to the ground. "How is my man Alfie?"

"I'm fine, Carl. You're up early today."

Carl made a grand sweeping gesture at his grounds. "All this stuff, I don't own a single clock, what I care the time!"

"I need a favor, Carl."

Alarm: "The tunes? Too loud, right? But, I mean, c'mon, amigo, it's Billy, right? Billy?" Carl lapsed into air guitar mode. "Billy, right?"

"Billy's alright," Aubry agreed.

But then apologetic, like a little boy caught doing bad. "But too loud, right? I get it, I get it, 's'ok, sorry, sorry, sorry," and he went to a scuffed and paint-splattered amp on the workbench, fiddled with some nobs and brought the sound down to something like an over-cranked car radio. "Better, Alfie? Better? No complaints now, right?"

"That's good, Carl, but that wasn't the favor."

Carl grabbed one of Aubry's hands and rubbed it vigorously across his ample belly. "I'm the genie, amigo, rub the Buddha's belly, make a wish!"

"Got a car off the road a mile south on the 201. I need it towed in."

"Oh, *ohhhhh.*" Carl stepped back, began to pace as he shook his head, frowning. "Jeez, Alfie, Jeez, I'm in it deep in Sophie Krebbs's fridge, she's got no fridge, no food and milk for the kids, ya know?"

"It's just a quick run, Carl --"

"Jeez, Alfie, Sophie Krebbs, ya know? Thing is, thing is, no fridge, the kids gonna go hungry, kids gotta have their milk, right? I promised her, Alfie, you know, a fucking *promise* --" Carl froze, as if he'd shocked himself, and turned the most pitiable look toward Liz. "Sorry 'bout the language, Doctor Liz, sorry, sometimes, ya know? Sometimes they slip out."

"I know, Carl, it's ok." She cast another glance over at the injured man who seemed as fascinated by her just-another-day attitude as by the Grateful Dead fan in front of him.

"Carl, please," Aubry pushed gently, "It's official, you'll get paid."

"Ah, oh, well, paid, paid is good, wear and tear on the wheels 'n' all, gas, mileage, all that, paid is good, who's gonna pay? Where's the mayor? Ol' Malley gonna pay? Where's he? That him hidin' in the Jeep?"

"That's not him, Carl, he's up at Moose Lake, settin' up his camp for winter --"

"For the ice fishing? Mmmm, I like that ice fishing. We go ice fishing this winter, Alfie? Me 'n' you?"

"You bet, Carl, but we ain't goin' nowhere I don't get that car towed in here."

Carl stopped his pacing, studied the injured man with narrowed eyes. Liz tried not to grin when she saw the man actually flinch at Carl's stare.

"His car, right?" Carl appraised. "The caped crusader here?" The injured man's shoulders flinched self-consciously under the draped blanket and flannel coat. "His car?"

"His car," Aubry nodded.

"Hey, amigo," and this time Carl addressed the injured man directly. "You wanna buy one?"

"Sorry?"

"Your car gettin' towed, must be dead, you want another one? Got some good ones here."

"Um, no thanks."

"Then maybe you wanna sell your junker?"

"Right now, it's evidence, Carl," Aubry said.

"Ooooh!" and Carl's eyes went wide. He hunched over, his gravelly voice hushed as if sharing some secret. "Evidence! Evidence of a crime! A *crime!*"

"Soon's you can, Carl?"

"Yeah, yeah, sure, sure, for you, Alfie, zip-zip. Sophie Krebbs won't know. You won't tell I took time off, will you?"

"I won't tell, Carl."

"Doctor Lizzy?"

Liz mimed padlocking her lips shut.

Carl frowned. "What about – Hey, where'd he go?"

The injured man had wandered off into Carl's mess of this and that.

"Yo!" Carl called. "Don't touch, ok? I got all this stuff catalogued right *here*," and Carl slapped the side of his head. "I know where everything is, ok? So, hands!"

The injured man held his hands out; a gesture of I'm-not-touching-anything.

"How 'bout that dude?" Carl asked Liz. "He gonna keep his yap shut 'round Sophie Krebbs? This dude? He looks shady to me."

"He's fine, Carl," Liz assured him.

Carl's frown turned to wide-eyed concern. "You hurtin', amigo?"

The man reflexively touched at his bandaged head. "A bit, yeah."

Carl nodded in agreement. "Looks like, yeah, looks like. Wanna buy a couple grams?"

"Sorry?"

Liz chuckled. "I don't know how he managed it," she said to the injured man, "but Carl here is actually a licensed distributor."

"An eighth of Gorilla Glue Number Four would do you right," Carl assessed.

"Thanks, Carl," Liz said, "but I think his brains are scrambled enough right now. Maybe later."

"I'll talk to you when you bring it in," Aubry said.

"You got it, Alfie, my man! *Mi amigo!* Here, hug it out, again!" And up in the air went Aubry. "Ice fishing this winter, right, Alfie?"

"You bet, Carl," Aubry grunted, trying to breathe inside the vise of Carl's arms.

Aubry turned back toward his Jeep, Liz following, but then they noticed the man wasn't with them. He was staring out at the corner of the field with junked vehicles, his finger up as he seemed to be counting.

"You comin'?" Aubry asked.

"It looks like he's got three, no four Jaguars out there. Well, pieces of them. *Jaguars!* What's this guy doing with four Jags?"

A small, sad smile peeked out from under Aubry's mustache. "That's a dream of Carl's ain't never gonna happen," and he let it go at that as he turned back to the Jeep. Aubry never tried to explain Carl, at least not to any length, and Liz had learned long ago to leave Carl-related issues where Aubry dropped them.

As they all climbed back into the Wrangler, the injured man was still shaking his head over the episode. "What a character!"

"He is that," Liz said.

"I'm wondering who hit *him* in the head?"

"An Iraqi sniper," Aubry said flatly as he started the engine. "We were over there together. I brought him up here when we mustered out. He's safe up here."

The injured man looked immediately contrite. Liz patted him on the knee, a way of saying, *It's ok, you couldn't know.*

But still the man felt compelled to say…something. "I'm, uh -- …"

"So'm I," Aubry said as he headed the Jeep back toward Morahan's.

Tell me all your secrets I know, I know, I know…

"Don't mess with my work," Liz said, batting the man's hand away from where he was fussing with the bandage on his forehead.

"Sorry," he said, "It itches."

"Then it itches."

He tucked his hands into his lap.

She and the man were sitting at the same table in Jocko's where they'd met. Parfitt paced restlessly around the dining room, Liz guessing from the pensive look on his face and the way he kept nearly bumping into the few tables that his mind was somewhere other than the dining room.

"Well, it's a puzzlement, isn't it?" Aubry was standing at the front window, looking back up the road in the direction of the crash.

"That your professional opinion, Alfie?" Liz teased.

But Aubry's mind also seemed to be elsewhere. He did his meditative side-to-side slow wag of his head, his fingers fussed with his mustache, made some kind of humming noise -- the sound of the mental gears whirring, Liz thought – and then, "Ya know what I'm gonna do?"

"No, Alfie, what're you gonna do?"

"Here's what I'm gonna do." Aubry turned to the injured man, speaking slowly, as if it was only coming to him a small piece at a time. "What I'm gonna do is, hm, what I'm gonna do is I'm gonna call Motor Vehicle, yeah, call 'em with your plate numbers, see if we can find out who that vehicle is registered to." A quick glance at his watch, a finger tap to make sure it was running. "Almost eight, yeah, they should be open soon, yeah, maybe that'll help us put a name on you. And then, what else I'm gonna do, um, what else I'm gonna do is I'm thinkin' of callin' down to Northern Light – that's the nearest hospital – call down there and have 'em send an ambalance for you. Whaddaya think Doc? Have 'em bring this guy in?"

"Prudent, Alfie, prudent."

"That a yes?"

"That's a yes."

"No," said the injured man.

"No?" Liz challenged.

"No. I mean, thanks, but no. I'm not going anywhere until I have some idea of what happened. I can't -- ." A decisive shake of his head. "I can't. Not just to me."

"Meanin' this supposed woman person," Aubry said.

"Yes, the supposed woman person."

"Nothing 'supposed' about all that blood, Alfie," Liz said. "*Somebody* else was in that car."

Aubry nodded, looking like he wished it wasn't so. "You ok with him not goin' the hospital?"

"No, but it's his call. Hey, Jocko!"

Morahan had been bussing a table after the morning "breakfast crowd" had left – all two of them.

"Jocko, do you think you could motivate Vi to make some breakfast for my friend here?"

"I'm not hungry, really," the injured man said.

"Your head hurt?" Liz asked.

"Quite a bit."

"Then you're going to eat. I want to give you something for that pain in your head, but I'm not going to be able to do that with you on an empty stomach. I tell Jocko there to drop twenty pounds if he wants to see another birthday, and he doesn't listen; I tell Alfie here to stop eating all this crap Jocko has on the shelves because his cholesterol is through the roof and *he* doesn't listen; *nobody* in this damned burg listens to me, so be a dear, dear, and be the one two-legged creature in this town that listens to me: have some goddamn breakfast!"

He seemed both stunned and amused by the outburst. Finally, there was a little smile as he turned to Jocko: "You heard the doctor."

"Eggs and bacon for the gent, Jocko, and a couple more coffees," Liz said.

"Hate to bring it up, Doc," Jocko frowned, "but remindin' you Mr. No-Name here ain't got a penny to him."

"My tab, Jocko, now phttt," and she waved him off toward the kitchen.

Then Jocko had a thought and froze in the kitchen door. "Hey, how's he want his eggs?"

Liz looked to the injured man and wasn't all that surprised when he shrugged helplessly. "Scrambled is always safe," and Jocko disappeared into the kitchen.

"Thank you," the injured man said.

She nodded it away. "Look, I have to call you something besides 'dear'."

That little smile again. She thought it wore nicely on him, but it never completely erased something around his eyes, a melancholy she was beginning to suspect had nothing to do with his current situation; some other thing that seemed permanently etched in. "I was getting to like it; 'dear'."

Liz mused a moment – "Let's see…" -- then grandly set a hand down on his shoulder: "I christen thee…*Adam!* Pending further information, of course."

He nodded in acceptance. Then, "Why Adam?"

"First letter of the alphabet, my friend," Parfitt said. He'd stopped his pacing to stand by the table. "Adam was also the first man. Biblically speaking, that is."

"Very good!" Liz said. "You must be hell on figuring out recipes!"

Parfitt sighed. "You get the work you can at the start. If I'm still doing this in ten years, you can put me down like an old dog and sell the meat because I won't want to live anymore." He pointed to the matchbook on the table, still there from when Aubry had asked Adam to empty his pockets earlier. "Hey, my newly-christened friend Adam, this was everything in your pockets?"

"That's it."

Parfitt picked up the matchbook gave it a studying frown, then held it up in front of newly-christened Adam. "You know anything about this?"

Adam shook his head. "Just that it seems an awfully fancy matchbook."

"Well, yeah, it is that. It's from a club: 'Champagne.' Down Portland."

"You know it?" Liz asked.

Parfitt nodded. "For the party-hearty young professional crowd looking to hook up. What passes for cool and hip in Portland. Anything about that sound familiar? No offense, but it doesn't seem like your kind of place, your kind of crowd."

"Believe me," Adam said, "no offense taken."

Parfitt set the matches back down on the table by the other man. "Here's the funny thing. This is all you have in your pockets. You have matches…but no smokes."

"No," Adam said quietly, pondering the fact. "No."

"Do you smoke?"

Liz held up a hand to stop the inevitable "I don't know." She checked the skin around his eyes, his mouth, his neck, looking for the wrinkles that went with a heavy smoker.

"Give the doctor a smile," she said, and Adam did. No tobacco stains on his teeth. "Pull your lips back." Healthy gums. "No morning cough, no raspiness in your voice. Do you mind?" and he didn't as she took his right hand in both of hers and separated the fingers, looking for tobacco stains between his index and middle finger. Nothing.

She noticed something else about his hand, and in a part of the world where the typical male hand usually had the texture of sandpaper, it was an easy thing to pick up on; it was soft. She picked up his other hand with one of hers, one of his hands in each of hers. The same; soft.

"Well, it doesn't look like you smoke. And for whatever it's worth, whatever you do for a living, you're not breaking rocks."

He seemed self-conscious about that; she felt a slight tug as he tried to pull his hands back.

"Not that that's a bad thing," she said. "I've known some quite brilliant surgeons with hands like these."

"You think I'm a surgeon?"

She smiled, shaking her head. "You don't have that annoying sense of godhood they all seem to have."

"Maybe I just forgot it."

"Maybe." She realized, just then, she was still holding both his hands in hers, and it seemed to occur to him at the same time. They both fidgeted, eyes wandered off as they each withdrew their hands, setting them in their respective laps.

Parfitt executed a tactful throat clearing to reset the moment on more neutral ground. "Adam, you mind letting me see your jacket?"

"My jacket? Sure," and he shucked off the tweed.

Parfitt went right to the label. His eyebrows went up. "Harris. Harris tweed. Take some solace, my friend: you're not poor."

"Ain't that just my luck," Jocko moaned, a plate in one hand, the fingers of his others run through the handles on two coffee mugs, "a man with money with no money." He set the food and drink on the table. "Wanted to ask you, um..."

"We're going with 'Adam'," Liz said.

"Yeah, well, Adam, when I saw you this morning; you called me 'Twombley'."

"I did?"

"Yeah, when I first saw you, you said somethin' like, 'Help me, Mr. Twombley.' Somethin' like that."

"If you say so. I don't remember."

"I thought I reckanized the name." Morahan pulled a crumpled sheet of paper from his pocket and handed it to Aubry.

"What's this, Jocko?" Aubry said, squinting at the gothic lettering across the top, and the blocks of text below.

"The deed when I bought this place thirty years ago. I bought it from some guy Twombly." He turned to Adam. "So, how'd you know that?"

Before Adam could open his mouth, Liz, Aubry, and Parfitt all chimed in: "I don't know."

Aubry's head was moving side to side again. "Like I said, it is a puzzlement."

Parfitt pointed out the front window. "There's your wheels; that nutbar with the junkyard's bringing it in."

Carl was at the wheel of a decrepit pick-up truck – Liz remembered it from the church grounds and would've bet money it was a derelict – hauling the Bronco with a tow bar.

"I gotta show him where to leave it," and Aubry headed out, scooping up a pack of Twinkies from a display by the door on his way.

"I saw that!" Morahan called. "That's goin' on your damn tab!" With a sigh, Morahan turned toward the kitchen.

Adam stopped him with a touch to the arm. He pointed to the two shotguns over the bar. "Those weren't always here, were they? I mean, you put them up, right? They weren't there when you bought the place?"

Morahan's hands went up and down as if signaling "I give up." "How do you know these things? 'Bout that Twombley guy and now this?"

Adam looked down into his lap. "I don't know," he mumbled.

Morahan shook his head and headed back to the kitchen.

Liz could see the frustration building in Adam. He looked at her, almost like he was pleading: "I don't know. *Jesus Christ, I don't know!*"

She took one of his hands in both of hers. "Take it easy. It'll come."

"When, Doctor? *When?* I feel so...lost. Unmoored. Do you have any idea what that feels like?"

"Not like you, but – ..." She realized she wasn't just holding Adam's hand but squeezing it tightly. And he was squeezing back.

"Hey, Doc?" It was Parfitt over at the front window.

It gave her a reason to let go of Adam's hand, setting it softly in his lap, giving him an "Excuse me" smile as she left him to stand by Parfitt.

Parfitt said something to her, but she didn't hear it. She was wondering what it was about this poor lost soul – other than that he was a poor lost soul – that had sparked a sense of connection with her.

"Doc?" Parfitt prodded, bringing her back into focus. He nodded her attention outside.

Aubry's and Carl's voices were muffled but she could make them out:

"You said I'd get paid, Alfie," Carl was saying.

Aubry offered Carl one of the Twinkies. "'N' you will, Carl, but you gotta fill out a voucher, just like when you do the plowin' in the winter. You fill that out, Malley'll approve it when he gets back, put his mayor's stamp on it --"

"'I don't mind doin' a favor for the town, Alfie, you know that."

"I know, Carl."

"But there's gas, the wear and tear on my vehicle --'

Which considering the state of the vehicle in question brought an eyeroll from Parfitt.

"Do the voucher, Carl. I got a form over my place; I'll even help you fill it out --"

"I mean, look, hey, I'm as good a citizen as the next guy --"

"I know that, Carl."

And so, it continued on as Carl followed Aubry back to the mobile home that was also the Constable's Office (or so said the hand-painted sign planted by the cinderblocks arranged as a stoop).

Parfitt nodded at Adam's Bronco. "You were closer to the car where we found it. I didn't see any mud where it went off the road, did you? Looked all grassy to me."

"It was."

Then, quietly, so Adam wouldn't hear: "Check your guy's shoes."

When she turned, she found Adam again studying the shotguns over the bar. Parfitt was right: Adam's shoes were crusted with mud.

Chapter Five

"For somebody who said he wasn't hungry…" Liz was watching Adam polish off the last of the food on his plate. "How's that food sitting with you? Feeling better?"

"Actually, I do. You were right." He looked over at the shotguns over the bar. "What do you know about those?"

"Question is: what do *you* know about them?"

He started to rub at his bandage, saw Liz's admonishing look and drew his hand away. "I know…*something*…but I'll be damned if I know what it is. This is killing me, this -- … You know, not knowing -- …"

"It's called psychogenic or dissociative amnesia. It usually happens as a result of a traumatic event. I would say a car accident and whatever all that blood in the car means qualifies as traumatic."

"Does it go away? I mean, do I get back what I lost?"

"Usually. But it can take anywhere from a few hours to days. Sometimes months."

"Great."

He began shivering again. Whatever comfort the food and hot coffee had provided was quickly passing. "Let's go," she said.

"Where?"

"I'm going to do something about your clothes. They're still damp. That's all you need on top of all your other troubles: catching cold. You," and she pointed at Parfitt and finger-waved at him to follow, "I could use your help."

When they hit the outside air, Adam wavered a bit on his feet and Liz and Parfitt grabbed hold of him from each side until he steadied.

"Ok?" she asked, and Adam nodded. To Parfitt: "See that house?" She pointed down the road about fifty yards, a small, bland clapboard affair, tin roofed like the other houses, but with a clumsily added cinderblock addition attached to the rear. "That's my place. Take him there, door's open."

"Don't lock your door?" Adam said with a cock of his head. "You're trusting."

Liz smiled. "Well, look at that: we just learned something about you."

"What's that?"

"You're not. You must be a city guy." Then, to Parfitt, "I'll be along in a bit."

Parfitt started to lead him off, but Adam froze, his eyes locked on Cargill's store.

Cargill had set out some open packing crates of different fruits and vegetables, a rack of T-shirts, some boosting the Portland Sea Dogs, others rooting for the University of Maine's Beavers. A couple of flannel-draped women were poking around the vegies.

It wasn't anything Liz hadn't seen every morning it wasn't snowing or raining, but it was bringing a slight, soft smile from Adam.

"Amused by the goings-on of the country folk?" she asked.

"It's not that. It's -- ..." And there was that look, again, of him reaching for something just out of his grasp. He turned and looked out across the field on the other side of the highway. The sun was up now, the open ground glowing in a golden wash, and far off was the glittering band of the Kennebec. Adam's smile seemed to settle into one of ease, of peace, but then, after a bit – as if some afterthought had prodded him – turned back to what was becoming a familiar, on-tap melancholy.

"You're remembering something?" Liz asked.

"No, not exactly. It's more like – ...a *feeling*. Can you remember a feeling?"

She offered a comforting touch to his arm. "We'll know when it comes back to you. And it will, Adam." Then she nodded at Parfitt to head on to her place.

"Just lean on me, friend," she heard Parfitt say as she headed towards Cargill's store. "And I promise not to take advantage of you in your debilitated condition. Unless you'd like me to."

Adam managed a chuckle.

"Ah!" Parfitt said, "Humor! First sign of healing!"

Liz thought – somewhere between a hope and an observation – maybe so.

Liz had learned in her first days in Warsaw, you might not be able to get everything you *wanted* at Cargill's, but you could get almost everything you *needed*.

Cargill's was the most general of general stores, shoehorned into the ground floor of a small house. Since it was a long ride to anywhere else, Cargill provided a little bit of everything. The variety might've been limited but everything from frozen dinners to fresh produce to cheap liquor could be found on his crowded shelves. Toward the rear were tables of clothing, and in the dank cellar lit by unshaded light bulbs, a motley collection of tools and small appliances and a host of other odds and ends.

The two women who'd been poking around the produce crates outside had moved into the store, moving listlessly up and down the few aisles with the flattened look of people who didn't expect to see anything they hadn't seen countless times before. They both had the same hard, lined look of too many harsh winters whiled away with cigarettes and beer and harsh husbands.

"Oh, hey, Sophie!" One of them was by the small, standing freezer. "He's got those Swanson Hungry Man's Vern likes!"

"Can't use 'em, Lil, not 'till Crazy Carl fixes my fridge, I got no place to put 'em. Hey, Doc," and she gave Liz a nod and Liz nodded back.

Royal Cargill – not "Roy," he insisted on the whole royal "Royal" treatment – was like a reverse image of Jocko Morahan: short and round, same age, but where Morahan was ruddy, Cargill was frighteningly pale; where Morahan's bare pate was covered with a few strands of wiry dark hair, Cargill's had a frill of downy white strands. At the moment, he was busy at the counter working his way through a pile of Twisted Bingo scratch-offs and Liz wondered – as she always wondered since it seemed to be how Cargill spent much of his time – if he actually paid for the tickets or was ripping off the state.

"How we doing today, Royal?" Liz said.

He shrugged without looking up. He froze in his scratching, frowned at the card in front of him – "Crap" – and attacked the next card with his flake-covered nickel. Still without looking up: "Hey, Sophie, got them Hungry Man's your guy likes."

"I just said I can't use 'em! Don't you listen? That loon crosst the road is still playin' with my fridge! It's two days he's up there playin' with that thing!"

"Just buy a couple for today, they'll be good you use 'em today."

"Ahh," and she waved the suggestion away.

"Men's clothes, Royal," Liz said.

"Left hand corner, in the back. Crap," and on to the next card.

As Liz headed toward the back of the store, she saw that apparently the mention of *men's* clothes had gotten the attention of Sophie Krebbs and her friend who were now doing an absolutely awful job of pretending not to be interested.

Liz grabbed a twill shirt and pants, guessing at the sizes, pack of boxer shorts, a flannel jacket. "I need shoes, Royal. I don't see anything. You have Carharrts or something?"

Royal sighed, a little peeved to be pulled away from his lotto scratching. "Got some Timberlands downstairs, I think. What size?"

Liz conjured up a mental picture of Adam's mud-crusted shoes, took another guess: "Ten and a half or eleven, I think. Some thick socks, too, case that's too big. And did I see some of those pippins I like out front?"

"Yeah, Georgie Pugh brought those in yesterday. G'ahead 'n' throw some in a bag if you want."

Liz grabbed a small bag from where she knew they were stacked under the counter, went outside and dropped four of the firm little apples in the bag. When she went back into the store, the two women were standing by the counter, hiding grins with their usual clumsiness.

"Got a guest, doc?" Sophie Krebbs smirked.

"Got a patient, Soph."

"Fella from the accident?" Lil asked.

"That's him."

"Hm," Sophie Krebbs said.

"Hm," Lil said.

It hadn't been three hours since Jocko Morahan had dragged her out of bed, the town had been asleep through most of that time, but already the town gossip line was hot with the news. Another lesson Liz had learned in her early days in Warsaw: CNN had nothing on small town rumor networks for getting news out.

Cargill was back with the Timberlands and a pack of thick wool socks. "All this on your account, Doc?"

She nodded, picked up the pile of clothes without bothering with a bag, topped it off with the pippins, then she turned to the two women, batted her eyelashes, kicked a booted foot up behind her, "Now if you ladies don't mind, I must attend to my beau!" and sashayed out.

As the door swung shut behind her, she heard Lil say, "She's kiddin', right?"

And then Sophie: "Jesus, Lil, get a brain, wouldja?"

From the first day Liz had come to Warsaw five years earlier, stories had regularly circulated about her, from the little cluster of homes around the highway out to the furthest farms. She knew this because no secret could be kept even from the subject of the secret when there were so many wagging tongues among such a small group of people.

They tended to focus on the possible reasons for an obviously well-qualified and skilled big city medical professional from a big city hospital in big money Boston to wind up in the Maine boonies. A professional scandal, a heartbreak, a heartbreak involving a professional scandal, and round and round the tales went.

She did nothing to rebut or stifle them. On those rare occasions she was asked directly what had brought her to Maine, she would smile what she thought was an appropriately mysterious smile, shrug, and say "What brings anybody to Maine? The foliage!" Or maybe she'd just carom into conversation-killing non sequiturs, like, "So how're the Beavers doing this year?" But people rarely asked. One thing she'd learned about Mainers: they might be curious, but you could be running a meth lab out of your cellar and, as long as you didn't bother anybody, that was your business.

Fact was, she thought the speculations were fun to hear, and they were infinitely more interesting than the truth. Someday they'd know the truth, and she was a little sad at what a let-down that would be for them. But there was one recurring point that, over time, had begun to strike a chord.

"She must be lonely."

She hadn't been at first, and not for quite some time. She was getting from Warsaw what she'd come for: a safe space. But at a certain point, it was starting to come to her that that didn't always feel like enough.

Sometimes she would stand in her little bedroom in front of the mirror on the scuffed dresser Carl had more-or-less refurbished for her. There were just a few random strands of gray in her loose, thick brunette hair, couldn't even see them if you didn't look for them, and the Maine weather had put a few lines in her forehead and around her eyes, but with a doctor's objectivity she could appraise it as still a pleasant face, one that had often been called pretty back in Boston, and a lithe shape that had drawn its share of looks.

But if any of the locals had thought the same of her, some time ago she had become just Doc Lizzy, and it was hard not to think – and it came with a pang or two – that this was how things would probably stay.

Still, when she toyed with the thought of leaving, maybe going back to Boston, or at least Portland… Nope, she'd think, not gonna happen.

You could, she'd learned, become deeply, comfortably addicted to "safe."

Size-wise, Liz's house probably qualified as nothing bigger than a bungalow, although calling it such gave it a character its plain, weather-beaten boxiness didn't have; even less so when taking in the bunker-like addition hanging off the rear of the house. The front room – what should've been a living/dining room space – she'd turned into a reception area although except for the banged-up, heavy wooden desk – another Crazy Carl-scavenged production – it still looked like a living room.

Adam was sitting at the desk, huddled under her flannel coat, Parfitt was propped on the desk frowning at the two people on the other side of the room on her sofa: Josie LeFevre and her tangle-haired, sour-faced ten-year-old boy everyone called Jelly for some reason that had never been explained to Liz with anything more than a shrug.

Liz dumped her pile of Cargill purchases on her desk. "What's going on, Josie? Why isn't Jelly in school?"

Josie sighed and shook her head, whatever patience and stamina she'd had for child-rearing having been exhausted by her three older children and a husband she often considered her "fifth child.".

"I don't feel good," Jelly snapped, sulking himself deep into the sofa cushions.

Parfitt waved to get Liz's attention. "You know what that little --" Parfitt tactfully cut himself off, although Liz had had enough experience with Jelly to fill in the blank with any number of expletives. "– that little twerp said to me?"

Liz looked back over to the mom and son on the sofa. Josie was looking up at the ceiling with I-give-up eyes and Jelly smirked at Parfitt.

"We came in," Parfitt went on, "and all I said was, 'What's wrong with you, little fella?' And you know what he said?"

"Fuck off, grandpa!" Jelly said and his sulk changed into a proud smile.

But that was enough for Josie to snap out of her resignation and slap Jelly across the back of the head. "What'd I tell you 'bout that mouth of yours, huh?"

"'Grandpa'," Parfitt muttered, shaking his head, and Liz couldn't figure out if he was more offended by the "Fuck off" or the "grandpa."

Liz pointed Adam to the pile of clothes on the desk. "I had to guess the sizes. Why don't you take those in back and get out of that wet stuff. You going to be ok on your own?" which brought an eyebrow-raise from Parfitt which Liz batted down with, "I was going to send you with him."

"*Quel dommage*," Parfitt said.

"I'll be fine," Adam said and shuffled off toward the back of the house.

Liz rolled the desk chair over to sit in front of Josie and Jelly. "Alright, you two; what is it this time?"

"I got a stomachache," Jelly grumbled.

Josie slapped him across the back of the head, again. "'N' no wonder. All he wants to eat is crap, Doc. If it ain't pizza or grilled cheese --." She shook her head in exasperation.

Liz shook her head for the same reason. "I'm going to explain this *again*, Josie: I'm a doctor, not a child psychologist. Short of sitting on him while you shove greens down his throat, I don't know what you want me to do."

Josie seemed to be seriously considering that as an option.

"I'm not going to do that, Josie, not even once."

"Um, Doctor?" It was Parfitt. He motioned to the landline phone on her desk.

She gave him the nod, then turned back to Josie and Jelly. "How about this, Jelly. If your mom agrees, as long as you eat *something* that's not beige Monday through

Friday, she'll take you over to Jocko's on Saturday and you can pick out one completely horrible piece of junk food as a reward? That's fair, isn't it? You do that for me?"

Jelly gave a surly but agreeing shrug and Josie gave an equally surly but agreeing shrug.

"Now get outta here both of you," Liz said, "and try to go a week without having to come in."

Josie pulled Jelly out of the sofa and started pushing him toward the door, gave him another slap across the back of the head.

"Wazzat for?" Jelly whined.

"Wastin' my time, the doctor's time --"

It looked like she was going to land another shot on his head, but Jelly dashed for the door. "You're gonna gimme brain damage!"

"I'm gonna give you *ass* damage you make me come back for nothin'!" and the front door closed behind them.

Liz sat back in her chair, a bit drained as these cases – and Josie and Jelly were hardly singular to her patients -- tended to leave her. She looked over at Parfitt, apparently on hold on a call, who had obviously been amused by the whole thing.

But then his focus went to his call: "Yeah, I'm still here…I almost hung up, how long did you expect me to wait? And do everybody a favor: get better music, that'd make anybody hang up…No, I'm not, I'm in some dinky little place -- " He looked to Liz.

"Warsaw."

"Warsaw. Never mind, point is, I'm onto something and it's got more intrigue to it than how to spruce up the family dinner table on a budget…Fine, fire me and I'll take it over to the *Sun* or the *Herald* and become a real reporter…All I'm asking is you give me the day to see what's what here, ok? Throw an old recipe in my space, nobody'll give a shit, you think anybody actually cooks this stuff? …Ok, thanks, you're a saint," the last bit sounding a bit sarcastic, and he hung up.

They shared an I-know-the-feeling smile.

"I guess we each have our challenges," Parfitt said.

"I probably didn't handle that in the best psychologically healthy way. To be fair to the boy, though, having had dinner with that family, part of the problem is Josie can't cook worth a damn. Only person I know can ruin canned soup."

Parfitt laughed. He turned to the county map mounted on the wall behind Liz's desk; a quick reference for her when home visits were called for. Parfitt stood close to the map, started tracing routes with a fingertip. "What're these dotted lines?"

Liz pulled herself tiredly out of her chair, stood with him to see what he meant. "Oh, those. There are a lot of farms scattered around the area. Those are access roads."

"Unpaved I'm guessing?"

"Yeah, why?"

"What do you think?" Liz turned with Parfitt to see Adam coming out of the hallway, miming a model's runway walk in his twills and Timberlands.

"Good God!" Parfitt gasped in mock mortification, "You've gone native!"

Liz had to smile; she'd been a bit off guessing at the sizes, but, thankfully, she'd guessed large. Baggy, she judged, was better than suffocatingly tight.

"I understand it's what all the fashionable types are wearing these days," Adam said with a model's twirl, giving Liz another reason to smile; the humor was a nice change from the man's usual cloud of grim frustration.

Liz finally broke into a laugh. "Here, let me make the ensemble complete!" She exchanged the flannel jacket from Cargill's on her desk for the bundle of damp clothes Adam had under his arm. "Now you have one of your own. For formal occasions. You know, like sheep shearing, ice fishing. Those special times."

There was a knock at the door, then another of Warsaw's weathered women stuck her head in. "Doc?"

"Oh, hey, Elsie."

"You had ol' Cargill gimme a call?"

Liz handed over the armful of Adam's old clothes. "Could you do something with these? Clean them up best you can."

"Hm," Elsie said, mulling over the clothes now in her arms, then letting her eyes drift not too casually over to Adam. "Hm," she said again. "Men's clothes?"

"Yes, Elsie, men's clothes," Liz said. "*That* man's clothes. Take a good look; I don't want you to get any of the details wrong when you gossip."

"Me? Gossip? Oh, Doc --"

"Goodbye, Elsie," Liz said, not so gently nudging Elsie back out the door. "Elsie does the washing for a lot of the single guys around here," she explained. "You and I are going to be a hot topic for a while."

"I'm sorry I'm causing you any embarrassment," Adam sad.

"Embarrassment? I'm flattered they think I have something steamy going on!"

"Ya know, I'm feeling a bit insulted I don't seem to be a candidate for all this hot lady's chat," Parfitt said.

"Well, you know: 'grandpa'."

"Funny. Ha ha."

Liz pointed to Adam and beckoned he should follow her down the hall: "Now! Come!"

But as they passed her bedroom door, he stopped. "Can I ask you about something? I hope you don't mind, but I changed in there," meaning her bedroom.

Remembering the unmade bed, flannel p.j.'s and clothes from the day before on the floor, she winced. "What is it?"

He nodded at the doorway, and she followed him in, Parfitt hanging behind, looking in curiously.

Adam pointed at the framed posters on the walls: "A Boston Pops Christmas: Life From Symphony Hall," one from Boston's Colonial Theater touting a production of *Evita*, another for a Van Morrison concert at the Boston Opera House, the Boston Landmarks Orchestra opening their summer season with something called "Rhapsody in Green," James Taylor performing at Tanglewood. They all had something in common; none of them were later than 2015.

He went to a bookcase, another of Carl's reclamations. He didn't have to list them; she knew the authors he'd found, an eclectic bunch: Roth, Hesse, Vonnegut, Asimov, Conrad, Updike, Marquez, Bradbury. He shook his head and muttered something.

"What did you say?"

"A cemetery of other people's memories."

"What's that mean?" Parfitt asked from the doorway.

Adam shook his head, unsure. "Something I remembered. Something somebody said to me. These books… None of them are new."

"Maybe it's your amnesia," Liz said, "but some of these guys have been dead quite a while."

"That's not what I mean. The *editions*… I don't see much here that's been published recently."

"You've been peeking."

"Sorry. I saw them, I was curious."

"Most of these were my dad's. He was a big reader. He passed away a couple of years ago."

"Sorry." Adam walked to the night table. There was an open copy of James Herriot's *All Creatures Great and Small* face down on the table near a framed photo of a younger Liz with a downy-haired, pleasant-faced gentleman. They were sitting side by side on a rail fence, what looked like pastureland behind them. "That's him, isn't it?" and he nodded at the photo.

"That's Dad," but it came out with a heaviness which even surprised Liz.

Adam picked up the book, opened to the title page. "This one he inscribed: 'Medicine is a science; healing is an art. Be an artist. Love, Doctor Dad.' He was a doctor, too?"

She nodded. "The book was a favorite of his. He used to read parts of it to me when I was a kid." Liz felt a sting in one eye. "What did you mean: cemetery of what?"

"Other people's memories." Adam shrugged. "I don't know what it means. Like I said: it was something somebody said to me. It came to me when we were over at that guy's place, the one who lives in the church."

"Carl."

"Yeah. All that…stuff he has."

She felt an unease, she wasn't sure why, but she wanted out of that conversation, out of that room. "We've got business," and she brushed by Parfitt in the doorway and headed down the hall.

The addition to the back of Liz's house had been built to house the nuts and bolts of her medical practice. Liz pointed Adam to the family practice table in the middle of the room. She brought the back up to a comfortable recline. "Sit," she told Adam, and after he climbed aboard, "Good boy."

"I think you've been spending too much time around the livestock, Doc," Parfitt said.

"You're probably right." She drew a glass of water from the counter sink, a couple of aspirin from one of the cabinets. "These are for your head," she said, handing Adam the pills and water. "Now roll up your sleeve; I want to take some blood."

"Couldn't I just work off your fee?"

"I want to do a comparison with the blood samples I took from your car. This may not be Boston General, but I can do blood typing."

Adam fidgeted.

"Squeamish?" Liz teased.

She was sorry to see that grim frustration come back. "I learned something about myself. You said it looked like I wear a watch. Makes me think it must've been something personal since everything that could've identified me seems to have been taken."

Liz looked over at Parfitt who nodded; made sense to both of them.

"Ok," Liz said. "What is it you learned?"

"When I was changing…Well…" He pulled up both his sleeves. There were scars on each wrist running lengthwise, two on each wrist, each maybe a couple of inches long.

Parfitt had stepped up for a better look. "Well, well. Can you tell how old those are?" he asked Liz.

"Hm?" She'd gotten a cold feeling in the pit of her stomach at the sight of the scars, and another feeling, something between sadness and pity, that whoever this poor banged up bastard was, his problems went back a lot longer than this morning. She ran a finger along one of the scars, lightly, just enough to feel the texture of the soft, rippled skin. That feeling of hers, it felt more acute with the touch. She pulled her hand away, hoping the feeling would go away.

"I said, can you tell how old those scars are?" Parfitt said.

"Fairly old, quite a few years." She pointed to the band of pale flesh around his right wrist. "A watch. But no ring. Or if you ever wore one, it was long enough ago that the traces are gone. You can lose a tan line in a couple of months, but I have a feeling…" Her eyes kept going to the faded scars on Adam's wrist.

"Not all married men wear a wedding ring, Doc," Parfitt said.

"A dog like you might not, but I don't think this guy."

Parfitt huffed. "What did I do to the ladies in this town? One sics her kid on me – Oh-oh."

Liz had pulled on a pair of surgical gloves and was loading up a stainless steel treatment tray with what she'd need for a blood extraction.

"I hope neither of you will think less of me if I avert my eyes," said Parfitt, turning away and going to a far corner of the room.

"Wuss," Liz said. She pulled a rolling table up alongside Adam for the extraction equipment, a rolling stool for herself. She took Adam's right arm, felt around his upper forearm for the median cubital vein. "Oooh, you've got a nice one there, Adam."

"That turns you on, does it?" Parfitt said from his corner of the room.

"I don't think I'm going to look either," Adam said and turned to face away.

"Another wuss." Liz knotted a rubber tourniquet around Adam's upper arm to raise the vein. She wiped the target area with an alcohol-soaked cotton swab. "Ready?"

"No talking. Just surprise me."

"Make a fist."

She tapped the vein easily and filled a collection tube with blood, then released the tourniquet before withdrawing her needle. She put a small cotton ball over the wound, then taped it in place with an adhesive bandage.

"There ya go, all —. Jesus!"

Parfitt came over. "Did he…? Is he passed out? What'd you do; *drain* him?"

Liz hadn't noticed because Adam had had his face turned away, but as soon as she'd finished with his arm, she found him slack on the table. She immediately went for his pulse. Strong; this was just a faint.

"Adam!" She gently pinched his cheeks. "Adam!"

It only took a few seconds for him to stir, blink his eyes open. "Oh, Christ, did I…?"

"Yup," Liz said. "Are you ok? How do you feel?"

"I feel fine. It was just… I don't know. I -- …"

"You remembered something, didn't you?" Parfitt said.

"The woman…"

"The one you say was in the car with you."

"Yeah. I knew her."

"How?" Liz asked. "Wife? Girlfriend? Somebody you worked with?"

"I don't know how, but I knew her. When I felt the needle, the pain… It came to me."

The three of them mulled this over for a bit, then Liz suggested Parfitt take Adam back out front. "This'll only take a few minutes."

While she was setting out glass blood typing plates and bottles of antigens, she could hear the two of them:

"Cigarette, Adam?"

"No smoking in here!" Liz called out.

"Jesus," Parfitt said, "Lady's got ears like a bat."

"You've got the same matches," Adam said. "That club in Portland. Champagne. You made it sound like you didn't care for it."

"Wellll, nobody likes being home alone on a Saturday night."

Each of the typing plates had three shallow wells. Using an eyedropper, she put a few drops of Adam's blood into the three wells on one plate, then did the same on another plate with the blood taken from the Bronco's dashboard, and then again with the blood taken from the driver's side of the car.

"You like it out here," she heard Parfitt say.

Adam, wistful: "Something about it…feels…*right.*"

"But you're not from around here. Your car --"

"If it was my car."

"If it was your car, going by the way it was pointing when you went off the road, you were heading north. No luggage in the car. There's not much up that way until you're a good ways into Canada. So, where were you coming from? Two-oh-one is paved all the way, but you have mud on your car. Matches and you don't smoke. Hmm, look at all the ladies out there pointing at this place! You're big news, my friend. Of course, it doesn't look like it takes much around here to get tongues wagging."

Liz took up the squeeze bottle of antiserum A and squirted a few drops into one well on each tray, then did the same from the bottle of antiserum B, then a few drops of antiserum Rh. She used separate sterile toothpicks to mix the antiserums with the blood samples in each well, looking for agglutination.

"What's your interest?" she heard Adam ask. "I mean, forgive me, but you don't seem like the Boy Scout do-a-good-deed type."

"Oh, believe me, buddy-boy, I am *not*! I called my editor while you were getting changed. Somebody else can write the piece on the tasty dishes of Canadian rubes. You're a story, my friend, and not for my rag. Your lady friend the good doctor might be happy to serve the peasant folk, but I wouldn't mind a step up."

"Ahhh, and I'm your ticket. Well, you've renewed my faith in the corrupt nature of the human soul."

"Cynicism! That didn't come out of thin air!"

There was a pause, then Adam, quietly: "It wouldn't, would it?"

And then Parfitt, almost alarmed: "Hey, what's he doing?"

Curious, Liz stripped off her gloves and walked to the hallway where she could see into the front room, past Adam and Parfitt at the picture window. Across the road, she could see Alfie Aubry walking slowly around Adam's car where Carl had left it by Aubry's trailer. Even at this distance, she could see Aubry doing his little head wag, a finger restlessly pawing at his mustache, then a thought seemed to strike him; he froze, then turned away from Adam's car and walked to where Parfitt's car was still parked in front of Morahan's. He bent down at the front of Parfitt's car, looked like he was clearing something away down around the bumper, then stepped back. He pulled out his notebook, seemed to be fixed on, by where he was looking, Liz guessed the license plate, and made a note. Aubry turned back toward his trailer, was about to go inside when he was struck again, this time by something about – so it appeared – Adam's license plate. Aubry looked from Adam's car, back toward Parfitt's, then climbed the cinderblock steps to his trailer, stepping slowly, his head wagging the whole time.

"Don't tell me this backwoods bastard is going to give me a ticket!" Then Parfitt noticed Liz standing there. "Oh, hey, Doc! Got a verdict?"

"Blood types don't lie. Blood on the dashboard is yours, Adam. FYI, you're O positive. But somebody else was at the wheel of that car. I'll call Alfie --"

There was a knock at the door.

"They know to come in," Liz muttered, opened the door to find a spindly little man with a face weather-beaten to leather standing there holding the reins of a swaybacked roan horse. "Seriously, Georgie?"

"Didn't know where else to take him, Doc."

Sure, Liz thought, *of course*, and she shrugged with a bit of resignation; after all, it wasn't the first time a four-footed patient had been brought to her for the same reason. "Yeah, ok, but don't think you're bringing him inside!"

Then Parfitt was pushing by her, pulling Adam with him out the door. "Hey, listen, while you're doing your Doctor Dolittle thing, why don't I take Ishmael here over to the bar. Sun's over the yardarm, maybe I can lubricate his memory."

"Do you even know what a yardarm is?"

Parfitt paused for a second, frowned in thought, then smiled. "No, but whatever it is, I'm sure the sun's over it. C'mon, Ishmael."

Adam turned to Liz as Parfitt tugged him at him. "Who's Ishmael?"

"Maybe it's better than Adam. He was a wanderer; an exile."

Then the two men were off heading toward Morohan's while Georgie leaned into her eyeline. "Hey, Doc, you get any a those pippins I left with ol' Cargill? I 'member you like those."

"Georgie, if that's your idea of sweet-talking me into looking at this nag, think again."

She caught the music drifting across the highway from Carl's lot. One hundred and twenty-three grains of sniper-launched lead may have scrambled poor Carl's brains a bit, but Liz had often noted how he yet seemed to have an unerring instinct for an appropriate tune as she heard Roger Daltry's distinctive growling:

Whooooooo are you…I really wanna know!

Afternoon

Chapter Six

There were a dozen or so diners scattered around Jocko Morahan's few tables; men in mud-spattered work clothes, a few of the townswomen. Some, Liz knew, had been there since the late morning, the farmers and farmers' wives mostly. "Lunchtime" might've been as early as ten for some of them as they'd been up since well before dawn. They came to Morahan's and loitered, maybe had a beer or two early as it was, maybe even a shot to shore them up against the autumn chill, but typically they were there because it was something to break up yet another otherwise empty if chore-filled day, and, for those on the more far-flung homesteads, it might be the only time they'd get to talk to someone who wasn't family, maybe even the neighbor who lived a mile or more up the muddy road from them who they'd never see otherwise

Liz found Adam off by himself, slouched at the bar, his hands cupped around a small snifter, his eyes locked on the figure staring back at him from the mirror behind the bar. Next to him at the bar, in front of an empty seat, were two empty shot glasses and a half-glass of beer.

Liz slid onto the stool on the other side of Adam. He flashed her a quick smile.

She nodded at the mirror. "Admiring your handsome visage?"

"Just trying to see if I recognize that guy."

"Any luck?"

"Not much." Then he smiled again. "You think my visage is handsome?"

She leaned in close. "Don't get a swelled head. The bar around here is set pretty low."

He laughed a little at that. "How's your, um, 'patient'?"

"The only thing wrong with that poor thing is Georgie Pugh can't afford to replace his worn-out tack. Some of his gear is rubbing ol' Walter raw."

"'Walter'?"

"First time he brought that horse to me, I asked him about that. He said, 'Don't he look like a Walter?' And, no, I don't know what that means. Ya know, when the phone lines don't go down and I can get on the Internet, I think I spend almost as much time researching the ills of domestic animals as I do on human ailments."

"You're ok with that?"

Liz shrugged. "Most of the time."

"But not always."

She shrugged again. "How many things do you know come with an 'always' attached to them?"

Adam winced, almost as if struck by a sudden pain. But Liz could see there was nothing physical about it. "What is it?"

"I don't know," Adam said. "Something about what you said…"

"You remembered something?"

"Not a memory. A feeling." His face went tight, his fist rapped impatiently on the bar.

She set her hand on his, quieting it. "It'll come. Patience."

"Can't tell you why, but somehow I feel I can't afford to be patient."

A moment passed, and it wasn't until Jocko Morahan was standing behind the bar asking her if she wanted something that Liz realized her hand was still atop Adam's. She asked for a coffee as she pulled her hand back.

Adam hadn't failed to notice; how long it had stayed, the suddenness with which she had drawn it back. She saw the question on his face.

"When I was at Boston General, there was another doctor, older gent, I guess you could say he was kind of a mentor to me. He told me I cared too much about the people I treated. I thought that was silly; how could a doctor ever care too much? It took a while, but after a time I understood what he was saying. Too many people come through the doors, and if you care too much about each of them, about all of them, eventually, well, you've got nothing left...and they're still coming through the doors."

"Is that why you moved up here?"

"Part of it."

"What's the rest?"

Morahan set her coffee on the counter in front of her. "Just so's you know, Doc," Morahan frowned, "your friends're workin' up quite a tab today," and he nodded at the empty shot glasses.

"I'll remember that next time you're in *my* place of business, Jocko."

Morahan grunted a philosophical grunt and went off to bus the now emptying tables.

"You didn't tell me the rest," Adam pressed.

Liz had been hoping he'd let the thread drop. She picked up her spoon from the cup's saucer, stirred her coffee although it was black and didn't need stirring, then said with the kind of smile that was a friendly but firm shut-down, "Stuff." Nodding at the two empty shot classes: "Parfitt's? Where is he?"

"He tossed back two scotches with a beer chaser --"

"He's a reporter alright."

"– and went off chasing a Pulitzer Prize."

"Without paying for the drinks."

"He seemed in a rush of inspiration."

"What're you drinking?"

Adam contemplated the snifter. "That's funny. We sat down, Parfitt asked me the same thing --"

"On my tab."

"– and it just came out: brandy."

"Hm, so that was tucked away somewhere in there," and she pointed at Adam's head.

"Somewhere."

"I don't know what surprises me more: that Jocko had something fine like brandy, or that he had an actual brandy glass to serve it in."

Adam took a sip from the snifter and made a sour face. "I remember enough to know this isn't very good brandy."

Liz laughed. "Ok, now *that* sounds like our Jocko."

"Either of you gonna want somethin' else?" Morahan asked as he drifted back their way.

"I was wondering," and Adam pointed to the shotguns crisscrossed over the bar. "They're Purdeys, aren't they?"

Liz and Morahan exchanged a look of impressed surprise.

"Yeah," Morahan said. "They were my dad's. When he was in the Army, he was stationed in England for a while, picked them up then."

"Do you still use them?"

"He occasionally makes a lot of noise with them," Liz chuckled.

Morahan gave her a frown, but then nodded a concession. "Thing is, I'm not much of a shot. I guess I do leave a lot of the rabbits laughing."

"Can I see one?"

Liz and Morahan exchanged another look; curiosity this time.

Morahan pulled a footstool from a cubby behind the bar, climbed up and gingerly lifted one of the shotguns off its mounting hooks. He handed it to Adam. "You shoot?"

"I don't think so," Adam said, turning the weapon over in his hands, running his fingertips along the polished walnut stock. "You keep it in good condition."

"Was my dad's," Morahan said in a way that seemed explanation enough.

"Late 1940s," Adam said, "or early 1950s?"

Morahan shrugged. "I guess. How'd you know?"

"Purdey only made side-by-sides before that. Then, they bought up Woodward & Sons. Woodward made over-unders." Adam smiled appreciatively at the weapon then handed it carefully back to Morahan. "You could get quite a good dollar for an item like that."

Morahan held the shotgun protectively close to his chest. "Like I said: it was my dad's. It ain't goin' nowhere but back on them hooks," which he proceeded to do. "You some kind of gun expert?"

Liz could see Adam was asking himself the same thing and see it in his face, that he was discovering the answer even as he was articulating it: "No, but I seem to know old things."

"And you seem to know them pretty well," Liz said. "Curiouser and curiouser, as little Alice said."

Adam nodded, as puzzled by the revelation as the others.

"Did Parfitt say where he was going?" Liz asked.

"I believe his parting phrase was, 'To explore a hunch.' Something about the mud on my car."

"Jocko, let me get another black coffee to go."

"I suppose that's on your tab, too," Morahan groused.

"Oh, for Christ's --." Liz dug into her pocket where she kept a crumpled wad of bills, managed to pull a twenty free and drop it on the bar. "Put that against whatever I owe today and please get me that coffee?" She turned to Adam. "So, as the gryphon might've said, 'Hey, Alice, feel like a ride?'"

"How do you know we should be going south?" Adam asked.

"Your car was pointing north when you went off the road," Liz said, "so wherever you picked up all that mud, it had to be further south than where we found it. He thinks so, too." To the left of the highway was a field of knee-high grass fading with the fall to a bleached out straw color. About a mile or so away across the field, bouncing along one of the unpaved access roads, they could see Parfitt's car.

"Here!" Adam blurted and Liz stomped on the brakes. They were maybe a quarter-mile past where Adam's Bronco had been found, by the turnoff for another access road leading to the right.

Liz looked the question at Adam.

He shrugged. "I just...*feel* this is it. I can't -- ... I can't tell you *why* --"

"Ya know, Jimmy Olsen is already further south. He must've scouted this road already."

"I know, I know. All I can say is --"

"Right, you *feel* it."

"Look, Doctor, if Parfitt didn't find anything, maybe that's because he didn't know what to look for."

"Do you?"

Adam made a wry face to which Liz could only grin.

"Alrighty, then, let's go with the feeling," and she turned the old Outback up the muddy track.

When she had moved up to Maine she had gone hunting for suitable transportation. She didn't want some tank of an SUV, but she knew the roads this far north could be rough and wanted enough room to carry her medical equipment. The dealer had a used Subaru wagon on the lot, told her the all-wheel-drive would come in handy. "Eyah, 'fore them SUV's got popalar, this was pracally the state car!"

She'd had enough practice on the back roads around Warsaw that the slipping and sliding in the mud, the bouncing through the deep ruts and rain gouges didn't faze her as she whipped the Subaru smoothly through its gears. In contrast, whatever memories were coming back to Adam, evidently the roller coaster ride of Maine's back roads wasn't one of them. He winced with every sideslip and teeth-jarring rebound while keeping a two-handed death grip on the handhold over his door.

Liz slowed so as not to splash mud on Georgie Pugh as they passed him plodding through the mud, leading old Walter along the road by his lead rein. The horse's heavy hooves barely cleared the ground, his bobbing head low in that way permanently tired old mounts had. The lead rein was slack; Walter knew the way and seemed to have little thought of going anywhere else. Pugh gave Liz a slight nod of his head, a characteristically reserved expression of thanks for not splattering. After she passed, Liz hit the gas again and almost laughed out loud as she heard Adam mutter a quiet, "Oh, God…" as his hands white-knuckled around the handhold.

The road ran up a gentle slope, finally evening out high enough to provide a broad panorama of the land around Warsaw, a view that ran out for miles up and down the Kennebec Valley.

"Slow down," Adam said quietly. "I think…"

Liz saw it; a small, derelict house to the left, set back from the road. She pulled off in front of the building, looked to Adam.

He nodded, climbed out of the car, his eyes intently focused on the house. Liz followed, carrying her Styrofoam cup of coffee.

It was clear to Liz there hadn't been much to the place even when it had been intact; a style-less, purely functional box with just a few small rooms. It had been beaten mercilessly by the years, the metal roof streaked with rust and rotted through in places, the glass in every window gone with the frames warping away from the walls, the once white-washed walls now measled with pealing, graying paint, and streaked with rain-drawn dirt and brown streaks from the roof. The grounds close around the place were buried in knee-high grass which rippled in the breeze puffing across the top of the rise. Some yards off, a pile of wood Liz guessed, from the sections still carrying a little bit of faded red paint, to be the remains of a small barn which had long ago collapsed in on itself.

It was a common enough sight. Liz had often passed abandoned houses, abandoned stores, abandoned cars and trucks, abandoned campers. They were the markers of somebody, maybe a whole family, which had died out, or maybe just went broke, or maybe just… Who knew? But the Maine woods were sprinkled with the corpses of dreams and hopes, some of them the most modest of dreams and hopes, that nonetheless had died out or gone bust.

From this high ground, in one direction they could see across the neat, cultivated squares of farms, left fallow and brown for fall and winter. They could see all the way to the Kennebec glittering like a diamond necklace under the afternoon sun, and beyond it the broad, dark shoulders of the Longfellow Mountains. Behind them, on the other side of the road, stood close, dark ranks of pine and spruce and fir. Beyond the house, an open field too neatly bordered by trees to be natural; Liz was thinking a one-time farm, a couple of acres it looked like, now overgrown with wild grass and shrubs. The field was edged by thick forest in a bold display of Maine's fall foliage; the bright yellow of aspens and black walnuts, the red and purple of dogwoods, the fiery orange of sugar maples, here and there a slash of solemn green evergreens, all of them, all through their ranks, seeming to quiver with their colored vibrancy as the wafting breezes gently swayed their boughs and ruffled their leaves.

Adam slowly walked past the house, and the almost glum seriousness with which he'd faced it melted into a soft smile as he took in the painter's palette below, raising his arms as if to physically embrace the view. "I know this place," he said quietly.

"You were up here last night?"

"I think so…but that's not it." His smile grew a little wider. "From before."

"Before? It doesn't look like anybody's lived here for…for years. I mean, a *lot* of years."

Adam nodded. "But… I can tell I've been here before.

"How can you tell?"

Adam turned to her and now there was something a little sad about his smile. "Because as I'm looking out there, I realize I've missed it."

Liz nodded. "It *is* beautiful. My dad used to bring us up here on vacations sometimes. To see the fall colors. Sometimes I feel bad for people who grow up here. To them, this is, well, it's just the way it is. They don't see it the way someone from outside does. The locals call us 'leaf peepers.'"

Adam chuckled at that, and nodded, understanding, agreeing.

She took a sip of her coffee, already losing heat to the autumn breezes. "I used to think we had a pretty fall in Massachusetts," Liz said, "But this… I told him, my dad, that I wished I was a painter because none of the pictures I took ever did this justice. He would say they're not supposed to; this is only for the eyes."

"He sounds like he was something."

"He was."

"What'd your mother think?"

She took another sip of her coffee, a way of putting off answering. "I don't know. She died when I was three. Cancer. I don't remember her." Liz smiled sadly to herself at the irony: *So, we* <u>both</u> *have things we don't remember that haunt us!* "So, it was always just me and my dad."

"Is that why you moved up here? For this?" and he waved an arm out at the woodland rainbow below them.

Liz found herself frowning, tried to push it off with a forced smile. "Part of it."

Adam nodded. "Stuff."

She went to her coffee cup again, took a sip, made a face and poured it out on the ground. "Yeah. Stuff."

Adam took a few steps down the slope, toward the open field, soaking it all in. Then he turned back toward Liz, squinting against the sun. "Hey, Doctor --"

"I think 'Liz' would be fine at this point, don't you? Since I'm calling you Adam?"

He smiled at that. "Well, Liz, I'm missing my whole life except for the last six, seven hours. You'd be being merciful filling in some of *your* blanks for me."

She weighed that for a moment, and it occurred to her it only seemed right, a balance. "Fair enough. Did you ever see the movie *Casablanca?* Well, maybe you did but don't remember. My dad loved that movie. I must've sat through it dozens of times with him. The Humphrey Bogart character has a line: 'I've heard a lot of stories in my time. They went along with the sound of a tinny piano playing in the parlor downstairs. "Mister, I met a man once when I was a kid," it always began'."

Adam nodded with a thought. "Ahhh, let me guess: a surgeon with visions of godhood."

Liz laughed. "Oh, *that* you remember!"

"Was he also the mentor who advised you against feeling too much?"

"I think he was jealous."

"Of?"

"That whatever I was feeling for my patients was taking something away from him."

"Sounds like kind of a dick."

"Kind of."

"So, you left."

Liz took some idle steps through the grass. Her toe bumped into a small, half-buried rock. She managed to pop it free with the toe of her boot, kicked it away. *You used to wear such nice shoes,* she thought. "That grated, but that wasn't what finished it. What did it was he laughed at my dad."

"I don't — "

"He thought my dad was a coward. Dad was a doctor in a town, well, not as small as Warsaw, but out in the western part of the state. Massachusetts can get quite boonie out there. Ellis – that was his name – Ellis said my dad worked there because he didn't have what it took to work in what he called 'the big leagues'. Said dad wanted to, 'Push pills to the rubes in Podunk' because it was easier.

"Ellis didn't get it. He was the kind of person who couldn't. See, in a place like where dad was – in a place like this – he knew everybody…and everybody knew him. He was important to them. They didn't just come to him with coughs and cuts. He counseled them, he comforted them, some of them he even brought into this world and then held their hands when they passed out of it."

"*All Creatures Great and Small.*"

She nodded. "At Boston General – hell, at any big hospital – they come in, you have them for a few days, maybe a few weeks, then, one way or another, they're gone. And for the time you have them, you have the administration in one ear, the insurance companies in the other, mostly telling you what you *can't* do. After a while, their faces blur together, the day after they're gone you don't even remember their names…and there's always more coming through the door. It's like a factory and you're one of those poor bastards who spends all day every day putting the same six screws into something. It feels kind of pointless. *You* feel kind of pointless.

"Yeah, I came here to get away from Ellis and all the other Ellises…but I also wanted to feel like the kind of doctor my dad was."

"That's a lot of stuff."

She looked over at Adam, his face now soft with…*something* that tied them now. Maybe, she wondered, because he, too, knew what it was to lose a past, the difference being she remembered hers.

They stood there a long moment, looking from each other back to the easing, soothing expanse of color and quiet. She heard Adam sigh, like someone wakened to a chore, and he turned for the house. There was a back door hanging by one hinge, so tortured by years of weather it looked to Liz that it might disintegrate at the slightest touch.

"Where're you going?"

Adam pointed to the house. "I think I should see inside. Maybe there's something…" and he let the sentence drift off with what she knew was a hope more than an expectation.

"Be careful," she called after him. "That place doesn't look too safe."

He must've agreed as he slipped past the listing door without touching it. Liz circled the house, moving from window to window, following Adam as he drifted from room to room. The rooms were, unsurprisingly, empty, littered with dry, rustling leaves and stagnant puddles, tracks of dried mud left by curious little four-leggers. It didn't take long for Adam to cover the few rooms, and then he was gingerly making his way past the front door which was in only moderately better shape than the rear one.

"Well?" Liz asked.

Adam's disappointed sigh said it all. "It feels like I know it, but…" A shake of his head. Then, like a hit from a mild electric shock, he went stiff with a quiet, "Hey!"

She followed his pointing finger. Standing at the near side of the road, maybe ten yards away, staring at them as intently as they were staring back, stood a white-tailed deer. No antlers; she's a doe, Liz figured, a young one gauging by her short snout, no more than a hundred pounds, her reddish-brown coat giving way to gray for the cold season.

"Don't move," Adam whispered. "She can't see you if you don't move."

And, indeed, the deer seemed to be trying to pick them out, her large, dark eyes fixed, suspecting their presence but unsure, waiting them out. She was close enough that Liz could see her nostrils flare, her tapered ears twitch, but the breeze was blowing toward the house, carrying their scent and sounds away from the doe.

Liz turned toward Adam. He was…*beaming!* Like someone given a delightful surprise gift.

The doe gave some unspoken signal and a small fawn, then another, then two more walked slowly out from the field to their left, their spindly legs moving cautiously, picking up something of their mother's wariness.

Then the mother's head went up on her thick muscular neck, and at another unspoken signal, the fawns bounced off to disappear into the woods followed by their mother, her upraised white tail flashing as it floated through the evergreens until it finally disappeared.

The deer had heard – before Liz and Adam had – the soft, slow *plop-plop-plop* of Walter's lazily flopping hooves on the muddy road, Georgie Pugh ahead of him with a trudge that wasn't any lighter or more energetic.

"How'd you know about the deer?" she asked. "To be still like that?"

Adam shrugged. "I just knew."

Liz held a finger up to Adam, as if to say, I think I've got something, and went out to meet Pugh.

"Georgie, what're you doing?" Liz called as she met Pugh in the road.

"Takin' Walter here home."

"I know, but why are you walking? It's got to be another two, three miles to your farm."

"You told me it was my bad saddle givin' ol' Walter here his problems. You said not to ride 'im."

"I meant after you got home."

Pugh frowned a bit, not at Liz but at himself for somehow missing that thought. "Eyah, well, I wisht you'da said that 'fore we left 'cause my legs're awful tired. Maybe you could give us a ride rest a the way?"

"I'd take you, Georgie, but I think Walter'd be a little cramped, don't you?"

"Eyah, could get crowded in there, but he don't mind ridin' onna roof long's you don't go too fast 'n' miss all them big bumps." He said it with a typical Mainer's deadpan that always left Liz wondering if they were at all serious…ever.

"I don't think so, Georgie." Liz pulled Adam over with a wave of her finger. "Listen, Georgie, you've lived in Warsaw your whole life, haven't you?"

"Hm, well, mostly. There was those three years in the service, spent 'em all down in Texas, not a fan of that heat, but with all these wars, I guess that was a good deal. 'N' there was that year less a day I did at Kennebec County 'cause a some *broo*-haha I got into with this fella over in Bangor – "

"I don't need the day-by-day diary, Georgie, but generally speaking."

"Well, eyah, generally speaking, I guess."

"My point is you know just about everybody who's lived here while you've been here."

"Eyah, eyah, generally speaking, eyah."

"Who lived *here?*"

"Here?"

"Yes, Georgie, here. This house. The house behind me. *That* house right there."

"Oh, well, that house? Hm. Place been empty a loooong time --"

"I can see that, Georgie."

"Hm, lemme think, lemme think. Hmmmmm…" Pugh's leathery face folded up in deep concentration, he turned to Walter as if the horse could give him a hint, then his face unfolded. "Was a family as I 'member."

"A family."

Pugh nodded. "Fella, his wife…and they had a kid, I 'member a kid. I forgot what that fella was growin' here. Beets or somethin'."

Liz smiled. "A son, they had a son."

Pugh nodded. "Eyah, that's right, little boy."

"Do you remember names?" Liz turned to see Adam standing closer by, his face…hungry.

Pugh shook his head. "Nah, this's a long time ago, years. I mean years and *years*, maybe twenny, twenny-five… That's a lotta beer through the brain cells, Doc. Lucky I 'member this much."

"Do you remember what happened to them?" Liz asked.

Pugh's face folded up, again, he looked to Walter, again, then back to Liz. "I seem to 'member…the fella, the husband, he died."

"Died?"

"Heart thing, heart attack, somethin' like that."

Adam took a step closer: "And the wife and the boy?"

"Well, she couldn't keep the place goin' herself, right? They left."

"Do you know where?" Adam pressed.

Again, Pugh shook his head. "I don't think I knew even then."

"Thanks, Georgie," Liz said.

"So, we ain't gettin' a ride."

"Heading back to town, sorry."

Pugh shrugged prosaically, looked to Walter and gave the horse a -what're-you-gonna-do shrug, then headed on down the road, Walter plopping along behind him.

Liz turned to Adam, found him staring at the house.

"This…this was my home."

"At one time," Liz said. "That's why you thought somebody named Twombley still ran Jocko's place. And that car of yours: the age is right, I'll bet your family had a Bronco just like that back when you lived here."

Adam nodded solemnly, muttered, as if in prayer: "A cemetery of other people's memories."

"Now, the question is, *why'd* you come up here last night?"

And now, just as solemnly, his head moved side to side. "Damned if I know."

While Liz thought the downhill drive would've been scarier to Adam – the slipping and sliding was certainly worse with gravity's contribution – the man seemed oblivious. Liz felt he was probably sifting through all this new information – Warsaw having apparently been his childhood home, the mystery as to why he'd come back – and only growing more frustrated as it refused to come together in an all-encompassing, clarifying answer.

They bumped back onto the 201, but Liz had barely gotten the Subaru straightened out when Adam pointed into the air near where his Bronco had gone off the road. "Wow! Look at all the hawks!"

Liz muttered an, "Oh, crap," and pulled onto the shoulder.

"What's the matter?"

There were three of them – large, dark birds, floating on six feet of wing in tight circles about fifty feet above a spot twenty yards or so off the road. Two more birds were perched on a large rock, its top just visible above the tall, waving grass, their wings spread wide to catch the afternoon sun.

"What is it?" Adam asked.

"Hawks don't gather like that," Liz said, and climbed out of her car. "Turkey vultures do."

She started wading through the grass.

Adam climbed out of the car but didn't follow. "So? Does that mean something?" although she could tell by the strain in his voice that he was afraid of what it might mean.

Liz stopped. The two birds on the rock folded in their wings but otherwise showed no concern as she neared, their leathery red heads turned to the side to fix on her boldly with one, unflinching eye. "One of us has got to move," she said to the birds, and when the vultures continued staring with their red-rimmed eyes, Liz charged at them, hollering and flapping her arms.

The vultures finally reached the limit of their tolerance for the interloper, opened their wings to their full extent and lazily flapped their way into the sky to join their circling friends.

Liz took a moment to prepare herself, already suspecting what she'd find, then made her way around to the backside of the rock. Tucked in close behind it was a body. By the long, brown hair, slim build, the shoes with a slight heel, Liz immediately saw it was a woman. She was dressed in jeans and a short leather jacket, torn here and there where the vultures had tried to rip through with their hooked beaks. The shade of the rock had kept the sun off her, so she still glistened with the remnants of the morning's dew. Red strips of scalp showed through the hair, matted with blood and dew, where the vultures had gone at her. She knelt by the body, turned it slowly on its back, gingerly, as if afraid she'd wake the woman although she knew nothing short of a Biblical resurrection would do it.

It'd been a good thing the woman had been laid face down; that had kept the vultures from getting at her face. Liz knew they would've peeled at the soft flesh of her cheeks, gone for the eyes. The woman's face was pale but not just from death. It had been obvious from Adam's car the woman had already lost a massive amount of blood before she'd reached this place. She was in her late twenties, possibly early thirties – the smoothness of death made it hard to tell. Pleasant-faced, dark eyes half-open as if drowsy. Liz tried moving the

corpse's head, flexing her arms, trying to ascertain how far into rigor she was. As she picked up the dead woman's left arm, Liz saw she was wearing a wedding ring; a dull, inner pain ran through her as the afternoon sun lit up the slim band of gold. The body was stiff and cold to the touch which coincided with her dying somewhere around the time Adam had stumbled into the arms of Jocko Morahan.

"Adam, I've got a medical bag in the back of my car. Get me a pair of gloves out of there, please." While she waited for Adam, she took a look around the spot: no blood trail, no signs of having been dragged or crawling through the tall glass.

The woman had bled inside her jacket, but Liz could see a neat hole in the leather, about as big around as her pinky nail, halfway up the woman's right side. She felt a tingling along the back of her neck; she'd seen enough of these in the Boston General ER to recognize it immediately: a bullet hole. She rubbed her fingertips around the hole: no gunpowder residue. Whoever had shot the woman had done so from at least five feet away, probably more.

Liz went through the woman's pockets. She could feel something in the jacket's inside pockets. She flipped the woman's jacket open and saw a massive blood stain running down her right side, then broadening at the hip of her jeans where it had pooled when she'd been sitting in the car.

She also saw an empty pistol holster clipped to the woman's belt. "What the hell…?"

Also on her belt, another holster, this one for a cell phone, also empty.

Liz reached to one inside pocket and found a woman's wallet alongside a half-empty pack of Newport 100's. She flipped quickly through it, stayed on the driver's license long enough to compare the bland but alive head shot with the pale, flattened face on the ground in front of her, and to get a name: Teresa Mayhew Dinsmore. Liz wasn't up to learning more just then, so dropped the wallet into her own jacket pocket. She reached for what she'd felt in the other pocket, found what she first took to be another wallet, then realized it was some sort of leather sheath. This, too, was something she'd seen at Boston General, enough so to immediately know what it was and now the empty holster made sense. It was a police officer's badge cover.

Adam was standing a little off the rock, not wanting to get too close. He held out a pair of surgical gloves, wanting Liz to come for them so he wouldn't have to come closer. She flicked open the badge cover for Adam to see.

"Detective Teresa Mayhew Dinsmore, Portland Police."

Adam's mouth went slack, he blinked as if he'd been slapped. "What're you telling me?"

Liz sighed. "I'm not telling you anything. This is her ID. The lady who drove you out here was a cop."

Adam started turning in circles, grabbing his head in both hands, looking afraid it would split from the strain. "What the fuck is going on? *What the fuck is going on?*" He yelled it, but his voice seemed lost and small in the empty field.

"At least now we know you're probably from Portland. I need you to look at her, Adam. See if you recognize her. Is this the woman that was in the car with you last night?"

Adam stopped his spinning, took a long moment to steel himself before nodding that he saw the necessity. He stepped around where he could see the dead woman's face, moaning when he saw her and immediately turned away. Liz thought for a second he might faint.

"Do you recognize her?"

Adam turned back to the body, forcing himself to study the slack, marble-white, heavy-lidded face. After a moment, he turned away, again, taking a while to answer, not quite sure of the right words. "Something about her… She seems…"

"Familiar?"

He nodded. "But I don't know why. If I know her, I don't know how. I don't know the name. I feel...like I never did know her name. How did she, um..."

"Gunshot wound."

At which Adam could only shake his head; none of it was making any sense to him.

It wasn't making much sense to Liz, either. Knowing what she had to do next, she told Adam he should wait back at the car. As he headed back to the road, she pulled on the gloves and unbuttoned the dead woman's blouse. Despite the extent of the crimson blot running down her right side, it wasn't hard to see its source just below the twelfth rib. She brushed some of the cakey blood away at the top of the blood spread to get a better look at the wound.

Boston may not have been a high crime city, but Liz had learned in her time that there wasn't a big city hospital in the world where, sooner or later, you didn't have to deal with some of the more miserable aspects of humans mistreating each other, and that included gunshot wounds. It was almost impossible to accurately estimate calibers just by the size of an entry wound, but Liz guessed at something typical; maybe a 9 mm or a .40 caliber, not unlike what she'd seen in Boston where the police carried .40 Glocks.

Liz had been so focused on the wound in the woman's side that it wasn't until she went to button her blouse back up that she saw the other injuries: four small bruises along the left side of her neck, a slightly larger one on the right side. She felt around at the front of the woman's throat, and where she should've felt solid bone, she felt something like gravel. A chill ran through her that settled sickeningly in her middle.

"Adam!" She could hear the strain in her voice, forced herself to sound more natural. "Adam, there's a blanket in the back of my car. I'm not going to be able to put her into my car, Alfie and Carl will have to come out for her. Besides, Alfie will probably want to take pictures. I want to keep the birds off her." While Adam rooted around in the back of her Subaru for the blanket, Liz buttoned up the woman's blouse, closed her jacket, then gently rolled Detective Teresa Mayhew Dinsmore, who'd left a husband behind her in Portland, back to the way she'd found her, face down. *Sorry, Teresa,* she said to herself, and could almost hear Ellis' caustic reprimand in her ear: *No sense bleeding for her now, Lizzie, the lady's dead.* Ellis had always thought mourning an after-the-fact waste of energy, and mourning for a stranger, an even bigger waste.

She heard Adam coming with the blanket. He held it out to her.

"What?" he asked.

She hadn't been aware she'd been staring, leaving Adam with his arm outstretched with the blanket. She shook off the mood, took the blanket and draped it over the body, tucking the ends underneath so it wouldn't blow away and, hopefully, so the vultures wouldn't be able to pull it off.

They walked back to the car in silence, but Liz found herself hesitating at climbing back inside as Adam started to slide in through the opposite door.

"What's the matter?"

She gave a meaningless mix of head nod and shrug.

"You ok?" he asked, climbing back out. Then he shook his head, reprimanding himself. "Stupid question." He looked back out into the field at the rock, then up at the vultures still circling overhead. "Seems sad to leave her out there like that."

"Yeah," Liz said quietly. Then, "Adam?"

"Hm?"

"This morning, when you told us about the woman you'd left in the car, you told us she was still alive, didn't you?"

"I thought she was. Looked like she was still breathing. I mean, barely, but still… Why?"

Liz gave another of her meaningless nod/shrugs and headed for her car.

Chapter Seven

It wasn't much of a drive to Warsaw but even in that short span Liz was sure Adam could sense that things had changed between them. How could he not? Liz's body felt tight as a spring, he'd asked, "Is there something wrong?" and she'd snapped out an, "I'm fine!"

The mood changed again as they rolled into Jocko Morahan's parking lot where there was a dozen or so cars and pick-ups parked there; a display Liz doubted she'd ever see unless Jocko decided to give away free food. Among them she saw Parfitt's car now splattered with the same access road mud Liz's car was wearing.

Liz made no move to get out of the car.

Adam sat there with her, both of them quiet, then finally: "Don't tell me you're fine."

"Ok, I'm not fine."

"What is it, Liz?"

"I'm trying to figure out how worried I should be about you."

"You keep telling me my memory'll come back — "

"That's not what I mean. What I mean is…" She didn't want to say the words, but they pushed at her. "What I means is if…I should be *afraid* of you."

She didn't look over at him. Like heat off a radiator, she could *feel* the hurt from him…then the anger. After a long, quiet moment, a tight, "Okaaay."

"There's a lot of missing pieces, Adam."

"Of which I'm painfully aware."

"And when I look at the possibilities…"

"Why don't you explain those possibilities to me?"

"In your favor, that woman detective came out here willingly; she drove, which means she wasn't worried about you. Unless you had a gun on her."

"A gun."

"Her gun's missing, Adam."

"I don't have it."

"Now."

"Yes, now. You saw something when you were examining the body, Liz."

"She didn't get behind that rock on her own, Adam. She'd already lost so much blood, the best she would've managed to do was crawl and I'm not sure she could've even managed that. But if she had crawled there, that would've left a trail, some blood. But, well…"

"Well?"

She looked around at the parking lot. Another pick-up truck pulled in, a man and woman climbed out and headed for Morahan's. *What the hell's going on?* But she realized she was putting off getting to the point. She took a deep breath, let it out in a long sigh.

"Adam, even if we'd found her this morning, there was nothing we could've done, she was already close to bleeding out. But somebody didn't want to take a chance she might've made it. You see…"

"What?" It had a sharp edge to it.

"She had bruises on her neck, Adam…like from a hand. Like this," and she placed her right hand on her throat to mimic the marks she'd seen on the dead woman. "Her hyoid bone was crushed. That's here," and she touched the front of her neck.

"You're saying someone strangled her after I left her?"

"I'm saying she was strangled."

Liz kept her eyes staring ahead; she didn't want to see the look on Adam's face. She heard his breathing; hard, angry.

"You thought I did it."

He went still, she knew he was waiting for an answer, but she said nothing.

"You think I've been lying about everything, about not remembering."

"Oh, I think you're telling the truth about not remembering. It's just that that doesn't necessarily mean you couldn't have -- … You just don't remember it."

"And since I was the only one in the car…"

"I am entertaining that possibility. And since I have no idea what the hell's going on --"

"Neither do I!"

"– I can't completely close the door on that possibility. You see that, don't you?"

She finally looked over at him. The sun had taken on a fall afternoon's bright amber quality, coming through the windshield at an angle forcing Adam to squint in a way which made him look pained. Or maybe he was truly pained; Liz could understand that.

Adam was no longer angry, not even hurt. The logic of it all was weighing on him, and even more the possibility that he might be responsible for the dead woman. He nodded slightly, debating her points internally, then forced to agree with them.

What pushed back at Liz's suspicions was…painfully simple: she didn't *want* this to be so. There had been some wounded quality to the man predating what had happened this day, something she was sure had to do with those scars on his wrists that tugged at her. Maybe Ellis had been right; she felt too much for the people she tended, and maybe that was clouding her judgment. But as she continued to run the facts at hand over and over in her head, wondering if maybe she was trying too hard to find a hopeful note…she found one, gratified it seemed to come out of the same logical processing as the more fearful scenario.

"There is another possibility," and she mustered a weak, half-convinced smile, "where you don't look as bad."

"Oh, for God's sake, please share it."

"Although it just gives us more questions than answers."

"I'm getting used to that."

"That woman's wound wasn't fatal, Adam, not in and of itself. If she'd gone straight to a hospital after she'd been shot, she probably would've lived. But she didn't. You gave her a reason to come here instead. It doesn't make sense that you'd drag that poor woman all the way the hell out here just to, well…"

Adam ran that over in his head, but he seemed struck with another painful thought. "That means she died trying to get me here." He looked over at Liz, the question they'd been constantly asking since the morning on his face: *Why?*

Liz could only shake her head helplessly. "I'm gonna go see Alfie, see about bringing the body in. And I think it's time he called the county sheriff. Maybe even the staties. Why don't you go inside and see if our Mr. Parfitt found anything on his tour around the countryside."

Liz climbed out of the car, took a few steps and turned back to see Adam still sitting in the Subaru, still running it over and over in his head. Liz gave a rap on the fender, bringing him out of his musing, offered what she hoped was a comforting smile and pointed him toward Morahan's front door. When she saw Adam finally getting himself to move, she headed down the barely graveled track to Aubry's trailer.

Across the way, Carl's speakers were pumping out the driving clavinet rhythm of Stevie Wonder's "Superstition." It was the soundtrack for dark clouds rolling in, portentous enough to make Liz look skyward, surprised that the sky was still a sapphire blue and clear except for a few scattered puffy white clouds, tinged gold by the afternoon sun. Hardly went with what she heard:

Very superstitious, the devil's on his way
Thirteen-month-old baby, broke the looking glass
Seven years of bad luck, good things in your past...

The dining room of Morahan's was as crowded as Liz had ever seen it, but few of the patrons were patronizing which she was sure frustrated Jocko no end. Rather, there was a concerned buzz in the room. Liz could only pick out bits and pieces:

"...maybe twenty minutes ago and *phhhhttt...*"

"...kinda thing only happens with the big snows..."

"…right in the middle a conversation with my sister-in-law…"

She found Adam and Parfitt sitting at the comparatively quiet end of the bar huddled with Jocko Morahan.

"All's anybody's doin' is drinkin' coffee," Morahan grumped. "You don't make no money just sellin' coffee."

"Boo-hoo," Liz said. "Why are they all here?"

"Phones're dead," Adam said.

"Don't know why they think mine's gonna work when theirs's dead," said Morahan. "Not like they don't all go out over the same lines." Morahan looked over the crowd and let out a peeved sigh, and he did it loud enough to be sure at least some of the space-takers could hear it. "They gonna hang out here, leastways they could order somethin' to eat."

"Mr. Morahan here says this has happened before," Parfitt said.

"Yeah," Liz said, "but in the winter, during a big blow. But a day like today?" She shook her head, puzzled. "Both lines out?" she asked Jocko.

He nodded. "I don't 'member when we lost *both* lines, even *with* a big damn blizzard." Then for Adam's and Parfitt's benefit, "We'd lose the line runnin' south, we could still call north, 'n' other way around 'n' such." To Liz: "But it's *all* dead. That's not normal." Someone called to Morahan for a coffee refill. "Leastways have a damn donut for Chrissakes," he muttered and waddled off.

Keeping her voice low so the crowd wouldn't hear as she didn't see any need for a panic: "You told him —" nodding at Parfitt "— what we found?"

Adam nodded.

"How about you?" she asked Parfitt. "How'd your 'hunch' work out?"

Parfitt shook his head. "I went down every one of those Slip 'N' Slides you people euphemistically call 'roads' and I'll be damned if I could find anything useful. Of course, I didn't know that was this guy's home when I drove past that house, but I didn't see anything there or anywhere else that lit any lightbulbs for me."

"So, we've got no answers," Liz huffed, "but it seems even more questions than we had when we started. I may not have a goddamned clue about what's going on, I don't know about you two, but I can't help but think this business with the phones is connected."

Parfitt nodded. "It do seem a little too co-inky-dental."

"Just a bit." Liz waved Morahan back over. "Jocko, have you seen Alfie?"

"I thought he was in his trailer."

"I was just over there. His Jeep's still there but he doesn't answer his door. It's locked."

Which made Morahan frown. "Alfie never locks his --"

"I know."

She must've been making some kind of face because Morahan's frown deepened. "You thinkin' maybe somethin' -- "

She nodded the concern away. "I don't know what I'm thinking. I'll see you later, Jocko."

She stood outside Morahan's for a minute, maybe longer, thinking maybe the brisk autumn air might help clear her head, let her put things at ease. But any possible disarming explanation Liz could come up with for Aubry's absence collided against the vision of the dead woman in the field. Eventually, the image of the murdered woman dominated.

Realizing – hoping, actually – she'd only be making a fool of herself, and preparing to pay the consequences for same in humiliation as well as repairs, she rooted around in the back of her wagon until she found her tire iron.

She went back to Aubry's trailer, rapped on the aluminum wall with the tire iron, calling out to him. When she got no answer, she told herself, *Ok, you gave him his chance*, and went to work with the blade end of the iron, first prying open the storm door, then the main door. Metal groaned, snapped, and the door popped free.

She'd been in Aubry's trailer before; the smell of stale food and unwashed clothes was familiar. No lights were on and not much daylight came through the towels hung over the windows.

"Alfie?"

She stuck her head in the door and called again. Then she took a step inside…

Her eyes were still closed but Liz knew she was coming to consciousness by the transition from oblivion to white-hot pain in her head; that and hearing Violet Morahan's tobacco-raspy, "Easy, Hon. Ya might wanna lay there a bit."

Liz slowly opened her eyes, and even that mild action seemed to stir the pain to greater heights. She tried to focus, saw Violet's doughy, wind-chapped face hovering over her, dabbing at her forehead with a wet cloth mottled with what she took to be – as her vision cleared – blood.

"Is that all mine?" she mumbled.

"'Fraid so, Hon, though it's just about stopped. Sorta. Wellll, mostly."

"Jesus."

"Yup."

Liz tried moving her head but that was a bigger killer than opening her eyes. She could see enough of the dowdy surroundings, the sloped ceiling telling her this

was a top floor, to guess she was in the Morahans'
bedroom. "What happened?"

"Wellll, seems you didn't take it too good, what
happened to poor Alfie. Not sure *I'm* takin' it too good.
Jocko was takin' out the garbage, saw Alfie's door was
open, saw you inside on the floor. Looks like you passed
out 'n' on your way to the floor you seemed to think it
was a good idea to bonk your head on the corner a
somethin'. You shoulda seen those three heroes tryin' to
wrestle you up the stairs. Those stairs ain't that wide, 'n'
either you're heavier than you look, Hon, no offense, or
all the three of 'em's a bunch a wusses. Wasn't for what
happened to poor Alfie, I'da prolly laughed hard enough
to pee my pants, but I don't feel much like laughin'."

Liz reached up to gingerly touch with her fingertips
what felt like the epicenter of the pain along her
forehead. Despite what Violet had said about the
bleeding having slowed, Liz's fingertips came away
showing fresh blood. "Crap. How bad is it?"

"Wellll, you're gonna have a helluva scar, Hon. I
tried closin' it up with some butterfly Band-Aids, but I
don't think they're gonna do it."

Liz winced at the blood on her fingertips. "Good
diagnosis, Vi. Could you go out to my car and get my
medical bag? I'm going to have to do something about
this. I'm also going to need a bowl of hot water."

"You gonna be awright I leave you alone?"

Liz nodded.

Violet stopped at the head of the stairs. "Listen, Hon, I don't want to be a jerk 'bout this, but could you try not gettin' any blood on the sheets? I only got one other set 'n' blood's hard as hell to get out."

Liz made a big show of holding the cloth Violet had left her to her forehead. "Do my best."

After Violet left, Liz sat up and swung her feet to the floor. It was a procedure that didn't go well; the pain in her head pulsed in an almost blinding way, she felt woozy, nauseous, thought she might pass out again. It was possible, she assessed, she had a concussion. She closed her eyes, willed a certain minimal steadiness over herself, slowly – *really* slowly -- got to her feet, shuffled over to the mirror sitting on the room's one, small bureau. She took the cloth away. "Crap."

There was a three-inch-long gash across the middle of her forehead, deep and wide enough that all Violet's butterflies managed to do was slow the bleeding to a steady ooze and make her look like something out of a Frankenstein movie.

She heard them – Adam, Jocko Morahan, and Parfitt – on the stairs, mumbling amongst themselves, coming up in a tentative way as if they were afraid they might be intruding. Liz was standing in front of the mirror with Violet holding a penlight from Liz's bag aimed at her forehead since the bedroom didn't have much in the way of good lighting. She had already cleaned her wound, numbed her forehead with Lidocaine, and was now stitching her wound closed.

"I didn't know you could do yourself like that," Jocko marveled. "Is it hard?"

"More fun than people should be allowed to have." Liz held out her needle holder. "Would you like to try?"

"Nah, you look like you're doin' fine on your own."

"Thank you." Liz finished the stitching, applied a gauze bandage over the gash. "Voila. What do you think?"

Violet nodded approvingly. "I was workin' on a quilt for Christmas. Wanna help me out?"

"We'll talk."

"How're you feeling?" Adam asked.

"Like I was hit in the head with a sledgehammer."

Adam touched his own bandage. "I know the feeling."

"Kind of like looking in the mirror, hm?"

Adam's mouth flickered in just the ghost of a grin as he nodded. "Kind of, I guess."

Liz dug a pair of Advils out of her bag and dry-swallowed them.

"How do you do that?" Parfitt asked, impressed.

"I'm a medical professional."

Parfitt shifted on his feet, as if he was debating something within himself. Liz caught him in the mirror exchanging an odd look with Adam. Then, "I don't quite have a picture of what happened over there. You what? Went in this guy's trailer, saw him and just, like, *swooned?*"

With Violet steadying her, Liz shuffled to the bed, sat, wished Parfitt would hold off on an interrogation until the Advils kicked in. "I saw Alfie, then I'm really not sure what happened. I must've passed out, clipped something on the way down."

"Uh-huh."

There was a doubting edge to it that rankled Liz. "What's your problem?"

Parfitt shrugged. "Just seems funny to me."

"You've got a hell of a sense of humor, mister."

"Well, according to Adam here --"

At which Adam seemed to shrink into himself and look away.

"-- you looked at that woman out in the field and didn't bat an eye. But this guy --"

"You seem to be trying to say something."

"I'm just saying it seems funny."

Liz got to her feet, wavered, she felt Violet reach out to steady her, but Liz shook her off. "Alright, let's run it down. First, if Adam had stood a little closer, he would've seen that, yeah, I *did* bat an eye."

Adam seemed to be trying to flash an apology to Liz, but she wasn't in a receptive mood just then.

"That poor woman out there wasn't my first dead body, not even close to it. She wasn't even my first gunshot victim. She also wasn't a friend of mine I'd seen almost every day since I moved up here. Maybe you'd understand the difference if you'd ever had a friend."

"Ouch," but Parfitt nodded, accepting he'd had the blowback coming.

"You want funny?" Liz went on. "I've got a funny for you. Seems funny to me how you missed that woman out in the field this morning."

Parfitt smiled. "Ok, I throw a dig at you, you throw one --"

"Not an answer. Do you not understand the question? Want me to say it slower? Because I can't think of smaller words."

Parfitt settled back on his heels, still had that aggravating smile, like he was saying; You want to play? Ok, let's play. "I couldn't know she was hiding behind that rock."

"She wasn't hiding; she was *hidden*."

"No difference to me; how'd I know she was back there? Look, I saw the car, I looked around, I didn't see anything. I wasn't going to do a grid search of that whole goddamn field. I thought the important thing was to find help --"

"We found her because of the vultures."

"Good for you. There weren't any buzzards on her this morning, ok?"

Which, Liz had to concede, was possible. The woman wouldn't've been dead more than an hour at that time, and with the cold and damp of the early morning, the postmortem body processes which would've triggered that radar peculiar to carrion birds would've been slowed. But something about what Parfitt said tugged at her. Her head was still foggy, she couldn't quite get a handle on it. She let it go. "Have any of you messed with anything over at Alfie's trailer?"

The three men looked at each other and comically as one, shook their heads.

"Good, because if we ever get police out here, they're going to want the scene untouched. I'm a little shaky on my feet. Could I get one of you gentlemen to help me down the stairs and over to Alfie's?"

"What're you going to do?" Adam asked.

"I need to look at him."

"Wellll, I don't think that's such a good idea, Hon," Violet said. "You know; it bein' Alfie."

"I have to, Vi. *Because* it's Alfie."

Violet looked over at the trio who seemed to be at a loss. "Well? Are you assholes just gonna stand there with your thumbs up your asses or you gonna help this lady?"

It was quite the little procession: Adam had Liz by one arm, then Parfitt, then Morahan. Liz stopped the parade at the bottom of Aubry's cinderblock steps. She pulled on the surgical gloves she'd taken from her bag. "You guys don't have gloves. Anybody who comes inside with me, keep your hands in your pockets. Don't touch anything. Ok?"

They all nodded meekly. She started up the steps, wavered on the first one, still not having quite shaken off her dizziness. Adam grabbed her by the elbow and helped her up and inside.

Even as trailer homes went, Aubry's was on the small side, a forty-footer. Every time Liz had visited, she thought; *This must be what it's like living in a submarine.*

The door opened into a living/dining area. The dining table was in a nook at the trailer's front end. Alfie Aubry had used that space as something of an office. The table was littered with paperwork, and he'd propped up a corkboard on one side, also covered with papers: bulletins from the town, the county and state, the sheriff's office, state police, the Department of Inland Fisheries and Wildlife. Some were so outdated and forgotten, the pages had actually begun to yellow. Among the litter of papers on the little table and along the windowsills were empty take-out coffee cups from Morahan's, empty beer and soda cans, on the table was an open take-out container with the remaining half of the cheeseburger Aubry had brought back from Morahan's for lunch.

Alfie Aubry lay on the floor by the table. His face was a mask of blood, his open eyes bulging, his tongue hanging out of his mouth. Nearby on the floor was his landline phone, with its cord wrapped so tightly around Aubry's neck it was almost buried in the flesh.

Liz must've been weaving on her feet, again, because she felt Adam's arm around her.

"You ok?"

She nodded. She could hear Ellis's voice, caustic, reprimanding: *Lizzie-doll, he's not there anymore, it's just a pile of meat.*

"You sure you want to do this?"

She shook Adam's arm off and knelt by Aubry's body. *Fuck you, Ellis.*

Her eyes began to sting and blur. She blinked them clear, took a deep breath. *I'm sorry, Alfie.*

There was blood along the edge of the phone. Aubry's nose was broken; actually, flattened. She felt gingerly around his face but there were no other broken bones; the blood had all come from the broken nose. Other than the wound to the nose, there were no bruises or scratches on Aubry's face or neck.

She moved to his hands. No skin or blood under the nails, no abrasions on the knuckles.

She checked out the floor nearby, looking for scuff marks that might indicate a struggle. That the floor could've used a good mopping came as no surprise, but no scuffs.

While she was examining the floor, she saw Aubry's notebook – the one he kept in his breast pocket – on the floor under the table. She picked it up and with her gloved fingers leafed through the pages. There were the notes he'd taken that morning when he'd first questioned Adam, but then… Whatever he'd been writing down when he'd been looking at Adam's and Parfitt's cars earlier was gone. She could see where pages had been torn out; whoever'd done it had been careful to tear out enough pages so that not even an imprint of what Aubry had written would remain on the blank pages. Liz carefully put the notebook back where she'd found it. She reached out an arm and Adam helped her back to her feet.

"He was hit with the phone first. It wasn't enough to knock him out, but it was enough to stun him, bad enough that whoever it was could use the cord -- …" Liz found herself unable to say the words. "He would've been in no shape to resist. No signs of a struggle. Whoever attacked him had to get close before making a move."

"It was someone he knew?" Morahan said, sounding like the concept was inconceivable.

Liz shrugged. "Maybe just someone he wasn't worried about."

"Why'd anybody kill Alfie?" Morahan said, still stunned by the idea.

Liz shrugged again. She turned away, leaned on the counter separating the cramped kitchen from the front part of the trailer. The small sink was filled with unwashed glasses, a kitchen trash can overflowed with trays from frozen dinners and more take-out containers from Morahan's. There was a frying pan on the stove, some shreds of days-old, scrambled egg peeling off the edges. Stuck to the refrigerator with tape were a couple of to-do lists, items only partly checked off, the lists abandoned long ago. There were some photographs: Aubry and Morahan in their hunting camos, brandishing shotguns and acting the part of fierce hunters; another picture of Aubry and Carl out on a frozen lake, standing over a fishing hole, both of them proud and marveling at the two-foot long lake trout that must've weighed close to thirty pounds Carl was holding up on a line.

At first she thought, *Wasn't much of a life, was it, Alfie?* But she reprimanded herself for the judgment. She couldn't remember ever seeing Alfie Aubry in a foul mood, his patience for the petty issues the people of Warsaw brought to him seemingly infinite. She would see him sitting in Morahan's, content to eat by himself, totally occupied with his meal, yet equally content if someone came by, asked to sit with him and pass some time.

Something about one of the photos called to her, she looked back to the one of Aubry and Morahan. Next to the refrigerator was a narrow closet for brooms and mops, neither of which Aubry owned. On those rare occasions he saw fit to do some cleaning, he'd always had to borrow either from Morahan. Instead, the closet was where he kept his guns.

He owned the shotgun in the photo with Morahan, and Liz had seen him with a hunting rifle as well. There was also the heavy revolver whose holster he could clip to his duty belt, but he rarely did so in town. He used to tell Liz the pistol was reserved for when he had a call to the far homesteads, "Case I gotta spook some pissed off moose."

The cabinet door was partly open. Liz went over, opened the door the rest of the way. Boxes of ammunition for the three weapons were on the floor, but the guns – all of them – were gone.

"What is it?" Jocko Morahan said and came over to stand beside her. He looked in the empty closet, made some kind of low, pained noise. "Maybe, um, maybe they, uh…" He was looking for a comforting explanation, and when he couldn't find one, let out that little, unhappy noise again.

"I'm not liking this," Morahan said quietly. "I'm not liking this at all."

"Nothing to like," Liz said. "We should go."

Morahan looked back at Aubry's body. "We gonna leave him like that? Don't seem right."

"Can't disturb the body, Jocko, sorry."

"Can we at least cover him up?"

Ellis would've said something caustic about how it wouldn't make a difference with the body in the trailer. *Not like the buzzards'd get in here, right Lizzie-doll?*

Again: *Fuck you, Ellis.*

"I'll get one, Jocko." Past the kitchen there was a small closet of a bathroom, and then the bedroom. Liz had never seen it but nothing about it surprised her: clothes on the floor, unmade bed, sheets with the limp look of having not been washed in quite some time, and food stains to confirm that. Half-eaten bag of Doritos in the bed, beer and soda cans on the night table. There was one, small closet with an open accordion door. Not much in there; Aubry's hunting camos, couple of wrinkled plaid shirt and jeans, a second un-ironed uniform…and a baggy dark suit Liz had never seen Aubry wear.

There was a small bureau with a mirror stand on top. Shoved into the frame of the mirror were several photos. Most were of a young, blonde woman, early twenties probably, plain-faced but not in an unpleasant way. And there was one picture of a young, shockingly well-groomed Alfie Aubry standing with her with a small crowd in front of what Liz guessed was some kind of municipal building: a city hall. Aubry was wearing that same dark suit in the closet. The blonde woman was wearing a simple white dress; the kind of thing, Liz knew, a young girl without much money could buy at a K-Mart when she couldn't afford a proper wedding dress.

Liz found herself having to sit and lowered herself onto the bed. "Jocko!"

Morahan appeared in the doorway. "Couldn't find a blanket?"

Liz pointed at the photos on the mirror. "Who's that?"

"Oh, that's CeeCee. Well, Cecila, but that's what everybody called her: CeeCee."

"Who was?"

"Alfie's ex-wife."

"Alfie was married?"

"Long before you got here."

"I figured."

"They also broke up years before you got here. Plan was she was gonna wait for him to get out of the service, they'd get married and then, well, I don't know they ever said exactly, but they were gonna move somewhere. She never liked livin' in Warsaw. Alfie came back, they got married… She wanted to go, he didn't. 'N' she never understood 'bout him 'n' Carl. I don't know any of us do, but we all got used to it."

"Where is she now?"

"Auburn. Well, that was last I heard. Moved down there after the bust-up, after a while she met some guy, they got married, had a couple kids."

"How do you know all this?"

"Alfie told me. Alfie used to go down there 'n' see her every couple weeks. You know; get coffee, maybe have lunch, just to catch up. It was never ugly, she wasn't mad or nothin' when they broke up, it just didn't work out. I think it was different for Alfie, though."

"How so?"

"I think he always had a thing for her. I mean, like *always!*"

"When we can, somebody should probably tell her."

Morahan made that little uncomfortable noise, again.

"Hey," Liz said, "don't look at me. You knew her, not me."

"Let's worry 'bout that when we get through this. How 'bout a blanket?"

Liz grabbed the blanket wadded up in one corner of the bed and handed it over to Morahan.

"You comin'?" he asked.

"In a bit."

"You awright?"

"I just need a minute."

After Morahan left, she dug the dead woman's wallet out of her jacket pocket. She pulled out the woman's license.

Dinsmore, Teresa L. Mayhew. Mayhew apparently being her maiden name. According to the birth date, she'd just turned thirty-one the previous month. She'd obviously not updated the photo in some years; the body Liz had found in the field was that of a young woman, but the license picture was that of a girl. Teresa had posed with that slight, awkward smile of someone not sure if she was supposed to smile for a license photo.

Liz went through the rest of the wallet. Some credit cards, Social Security card, insurance card, card for the Portland P.D.'s credit union, sixty-two dollars in assorted bills.

There was a pocket behind the credit card holders. Liz found two small photos in there.

The first showed a young Teresa in a crisp police uniform with a man about her age in an equally virgin-looking uniform, both beaming smiles verging on a laugh, arms around each other. In the background, other policemen and policewomen mingling with civilians – family? -- balloons and banners. Liz turned the photo over. In neat, graceful print:

Criminal Justice Academy Graduation

and a date seven years earlier.

The second photo showed the same couple, maybe around the same time since they looked no older, in bathing suits on a beach. They were squinting into an amber-flavored afternoon light, huddled up against each other, showing the same giddy, open-mouthed smiles, each holding their left hand toward the camera showing off wedding bands which flared in the bright sun. In the background Liz could see other bathers, behind them a pier crowded with little shops running about fifty yards into the shallow surf, and off to the left a Ferris wheel. Liz recognized it as Old Orchard Beach and she knew she was looking at a honeymoon for a couple who couldn't afford much more.

She looked from Teresa's photos to the pictures Alfie Aubry had wedged into the frame of his mirror and felt a heaviness that made her want to fall back on Aubry's bed, close her eyes, and let the world go on its own, horrible, tragedy-ridden way.

This was what Ellis never understood. Or didn't care to. That all those bodies they treated in Boston General, the diseased and broken, the traumatized and abused...they were all connected to other people: family, friends, parents, children, grandchildren, grandparents. When you treated someone who was hurt, all those people connected to that person hurt in some way. And when they died, something in those other people died, too.

She could easily picture how Ellis would've dealt with an Adam stumbling into the Boston General ER. "Stick a Band-Aid on his head, Lizzie-doll, call for a psych eval and let the nut handlers deal with him." He wouldn't've cared or even let it enter his head that somewhere in Boston, a wife, a parent, a child might be wondering what had happened to their husband, their son, their dad. Or that Adam might be wondering if there was a wife, a mom or dad, a son or daughter worried and waiting somewhere for him.

Those scars on Adam's wrists? "Old, not our business," Ellis would've said. The way Adam touched a non-existent ring? "I don't care if he's touching a non-existent dog collar on his neck. Stitch up his head and after that, either boot him to the curb or kick him upstairs to the Psych Ward but, Lizzie-doll, once the bleeding stops, *we* are *done!* We are *not* the lost-and-found, Sweet-cheeks."

But thinking about those scars, Liz wondered if she'd be doing Adam any favors bringing him back in touch with whatever was behind them.

There were times – then and now, and this was one of them – when she thought, or at least wondered if, Ellis might've been right, at least to some degree. If you felt all that pain along with them, grieved a loss along with them, how much of that could you carry before it broke you? She knew, although she'd never admitted it to anyone, that part of the driver for coming to little Warsaw, out beyond the gnat-like annoyance of cell phones, where the only news was the gossip network concerning the locals and the outside world might as well not exist, wasn't just to be a doctor where doctoring made a difference, as it had with her dad; but to find a place where the flow of shared pain was manageable and bearable because it was not in her to be an Ellis; to cauterize the nerve endings of the heart and address every ailing, dying person as a bag of meat disassociated from those fretting, weeping people in the waiting room.

"Doc?"

It was Morahan.

She slid Teresa Dinsmore's photos back into their home in her wallet, dropped the wallet back in her jacket pocket. "I'm ok."

"It's not that…"

She looked up and saw Morahan fidgeting in the narrow doorway. She looked the question at him: *what?*

"I just thought of somethin'."

"Ok."

"Somebody's gonna have to tell Carl…'bout Alfie."

"Shit."

"I know I know him longer, Doc, it's just… I gotta be honest; I don't know how to do it. You know; it's *Carl*."

Liz nodded. "I'll do it."

She followed Morahan out of the bedroom. Parfitt and Adam were already outside. She stopped, looked at the blanket-covered figure on the floor of the dining nook. Morahan waited for her in the entrance door.

"Doc?"

She nodded. *I don't know how you did it, Ellis…but I can't.*

She wiped at a bit of moisture in the corner of one eye, then followed Morahan outside.

Chapter Eight

Carl stared at the floor, at the ceiling, looked all around his home in the old church like it was possible to find something that would explain, clarify. It wasn't there. He shook his head. "I don't, I don't, ya know…I…I don't *understand*."

Liz knew Carl meant it literally, that his poor, bullet-addled brain couldn't make sense of the news Liz had delivered.

They were sitting in one of the few pews Carl had left in place at the back of the church when he'd moved in. "Guests gotta have a place to sit," was how he'd explained it to Liz the first time she'd been inside years ago. As for the rest of the space…

Carl had pulled out most of the pews – Liz had seen a few piled up in a far end of Carl's lot, overgrown with vines and weeds – leaving the rest of the nave open and bare. There was a certain, blunt functionality to the space; things were there because they needed to be, with no care or sensibility beyond that. Plopped in the middle of the space was a four-poster bed, the brass posters tarnished and spotted; Carl had no doubt salvaged it like everything else he owned and sold. A wooden crate served as a night table. In another part of the space was a sagging sofa with bricks for legs, it's tattered upholstery sloppily covered with an equally tattered quilt. Against one wall, a wood-burning stove for cooking and heat. And along the walls and up on the raised floor of the sanctuary were worktables – some made of odd pieces of lumber hammered together, others no more than a plywood sheet thrown across sawhorses – littered with half disassembled appliances, small pieces of furniture partway through some kind of rough refurbishing, electronics with their guts spilled out across the tabletop. It was, Liz thought, a perfect reflection of the chaos interrupted by instances of clearly focused activity that was Carl's damaged psyche.

Carl slowly rose from the pew, walked out into what was left of the church's main aisle, then came back to his seat, still shaking his head. But the confusion in his face had been replaced with a kind of pain – something that cut to the core of the man – Liz had never seen before, not in all the anguished waiting room faces she'd seen back in Boston.

"I…I…I.."

"I know Carl."

"Who would hurt Alfie, Doctor Lizzie? I mean…*Alfie!*"

"I don't know, Carl. But we'll find out."

"*Alfie!*"

Liz took one of Carl's calloused bearpaw-sized hands between hers. He gripped her back so tightly it almost hurt.

"We were gonna, 'member we were saying this morning? We were gonna go ice fishing this winter, me 'n' Alfie, 'member?"

Liz nodded. "I remember."

"He was my friend, Doctor Lizzie."

"He was my friend, too, Carl. He was everybody's friend."

"Yeah, but...but...I mean..." His dark, almost childlike eyes darted this way and that as he tried to find the words. "Doctor Lizzie, Alfie was my *friend*...ya know?"

"I know." And she did. It was a word that meant something different for Carl; the word he had to use because there was no word.

And then his face sagged, the whole of the big man sagged, and he looked lost as his eyes grew wet. "What am I gonna do, Doctor Lizzie? I dunno, I dunno what I'm gonna do."

"Why don't you come over to Jocko's with me, Carl? Just so you're not alone right now. At least for a little while."

"Hm?" He hadn't heard.

She forced calm into her voice; she didn't want Carl to know how worried she was about what that kind of monumental grief might push him to. "Come to Jocko's with me. We were all friends with Alfie. We'll sit together."

Carl took a deep breath, his body grew solid, again. He pulled his hand away from hers, stood, went back into the aisle, looked from one worktable to another as if assessing priorities. "No no no, I got, I got stuff I gotta do, I got, ya know, all this stuff, Sophie Krebbs's fridge 'n' stuff, she's been waitin' for…I got, I got…*stuff*…"

He went over to one work bench where there was an ancient eight-track player. He rifled through a pile of cartridges, slipped one in, then started poking through the bits of copper piping and fittings on the bench. From the player's speaker, the old tape warbling: Elton John's "Where to Now, Saint Peter."

Liz walked over to him but left him the kind of space she thought he wanted. "Are you going to be ok, Carl?"

"Stuff to do, Doctor Lizzie, I'll be busy, busy, busy, busy…"

"Listen to me, Carl. Are you listening?"

A bare nod.

"If you start feeling bad, I mean really bad, promise me you'll come over to Jocko's, ok? You feel bad and don't feel like working on stuff anymore, you come over to us. We're your friends, too, Carl."

"Mm."

"Carl?"

A hardly audible grunt.

"Ok, then, we'll be there for you." She turned for the double doors leading outside, not wanting to leave Carl – ol' Crazy Carl – alone, but not thinking of anything else she could do, anything else to say.

Then, as she reached for the door, Carl called out to her without looking up from his work: "Doctor Lizzie?"

"Yeah, Carl?"

"Why would anybody wanna hurt my friend Alfie?"

"I don't know, Carl."

"Listen, Doctor Lizzie, if you find 'em, you tell me, ok?" And now he looked over to her, and Liz felt her throat tighten as she saw Carl's eyes: two dark, cold, bottomless holes.

She could only muster a nod, then turned for the door, the plaintive, wavering music echoing around the great empty space of the church…

This lazy life is short. Something for nothing always ending.

Jocko Morahan refilled her cup of coffee. Liz cradled the cup, taking the warmth, trying to shake off the chill she'd had ever since she'd left Carl.

"How'd he take it?" Morahan asked.

Liz shrugged. Explaining anything about Carl always defied words. All she could come up with was, "He hurts."

Morahan nodded, seeming to understand the said and unsaid. He turned to Parfitt. "You goin' for another?"

Liz was sitting with Adam and Parfitt at a table tucked in a corner of Morahan's dining room. Most of the crowd had gone home, realizing there was nothing to accomplish about the phone situation at Morahan's, and brooding over the news about Alfie Aubry. They would go back to their homes, Liz thought, lock doors they had never locked, and the hunting rifles would come off their wall racks.

Morahan was pointing at the empty whisky tumbler in front of Parfitt.

Before Parfitt could say anything, Liz cleared her throat. "*You're* paying for those, just so you know."

Parfitt put on a look of being hurt. "Harsh! I guess the honeymoon's over."

"Buddy-boy, we skipped from not-dating right to divorce."

Parfitt held up his hands in surrender. "Look, I get it, I'd be ticked off, too. I didn't mean anything when I was wondering if you, well, you know. I didn't know the cop, constable, whatever he is, was, I didn't know he was some old friend of yours. Hey, I don't know who you people are, I don't know who's friends with who --"

Liz gave him a sharp look. "If I were you, I'd shut up before you dig your hole deeper."

"Can I apologize?"

"Sure. It won't do any good, but you can."

Parfitt held up a finger, struck with an idea. "I think maybe I can make it up to you."

Liz looked to Adam. "This is going to be good."

Adam smiled at that.

"Make it up to *all* of you," Parfitt said. "Here's what I'm thinking. I'm thinking somebody should go for help." Parfitt finished with a dramatic pause, his face a big, semaphored *Well? What do you think?*

Liz couldn't help but smile. She took a sip of her coffee, set the cup down, slowly twirled it around on its saucer. "So, I understand," she said musingly, "You not only want to write this award-winning journalistic coup, you want to be the hero in it, too?" She shook her head. Without knowing Parfitt well or long, the egocentricity of it still seemed *so* him!

"I'm not looking to be a hero," he said with a horrible pretense of modesty.

"Good," Liz said, "because it's not a good fit on you."

Parfitt winced. "Gimme a break, Doc, huh? I figure I drive south until I hit a cell service area and get some police in here."

"You'll hit a town 'fore that," Morahan said, "maybe thirty, forty minutes, depending on how heavy a foot you got on the gas."

"In that case," Parfitt said, "I could probably make it in twenty." He clomped a foot heavy on the floor. "Size eleven and heavy as hell."

Liz took another musing sip of her coffee. "I don't want to piss on your parade, John Wayne --"

"The hell you don't."

It was hard for Liz not to grin because Parfitt wasn't wrong. "– but Community Phone undoubtedly already knows service is down and probably has a crew on the road as we speak. And I'm sure Sergeant Dinsmore's husband has been wondering why his wife didn't come home last night; the Portland police may already be out looking for her."

Parfitt gave a perfunctory nod; *Yeah, I've considered all that, but...* "I still think it's worth a shot."

Liz looked over to Adam, trying to get a read on his thinking. He looked noncommittal, keeping a low profile, Liz guessing he was still feeling a bit guilty about being party to Parfitt's allegations earlier. She turned back to Parfitt. "As a physician sworn to 'do no harm,' I feel obligated to point out certain health hazards, like whoever is behind this has already killed two people, cut the phone lines… Has it occurred to you they might be looking for someone to try something like this?"

Parfitt gave her an aggravating smile, batting his eyelashes in even more aggravating fashion. "Oh, so you still care!"

"Not really. Hippocratic Oath and all that."

Parfitt turned serious. "So far, I haven't seen anything that looks like this is more than one person at work, and I figure that one person is going to have eyes on *him*," and he nodded at Adam. "If he stays, they'll stay."

"Not much comfort for me," Adam said.

Parfitt gave a *too bad* shrug. "Point is, I should have an open road out."

"And if there is more than one person?" Liz asked.

Parfitt sighed. "Well then, I'm probably screwed, but it seems like a reasonable bet to me. Look, I've got a self-preservation thing. Like you said, two people are dead, we don't know why, and I've got this real selfish desire not to wind up added to that list."

Liz nodded, understanding. "So, you're not so much going for help as jumping ship."

"Well, that's not how I'd put it…"

"I'm sure. But that I can buy." She pointed at his drink. "*You're* still paying for that."

Parfitt downed the drink, stood, dropped a few bills on the table – "That should include a generous gratuity for you, innkeeper!" – then struck a pose, flexed at the knees like a fencer, one arm and pointing finger leveled at the door. "Thus, with his courage fortified, our intrepid seeker of all true things embarks on his mission of rescue and salvation!"

Liz gave a few lazy claps. "That was good."

Partfitt grinned. "I thought so," and headed out toward his car.

Morahan flicked through the cash Parfitt had left on the table. "Generous gratuity my ass; the sonofabitch is short."

Some of the things that had been tugging at Liz since the morning started tugging again. She got to her feet, went to the front window to watch Parfitt climb into his car – splattered with mud from its bouncing around the access roads -- and drive off, heading south on the 201.

"Shit…"

She hadn't heard Adam come stand beside her. She looked to him, then to Parfitt's car disappearing down the highway and sighed.

"What?" Adam asked.

"I wouldn't hold my breath he's bringing back help."

Liz took a pause outside of Morahan's. She pulled her jacket close around her; the late afternoon was growing chilly. To the west, the sun was sinking over the Longfellows, more orange than yellow. Overhead Liz could see light brushes of orange against a darkening blue sky, shading into a fiery orange-red toward the eastern horizon.

She heard the bell over Morahan's door and Adam was standing beside her. "What did you mean by that? About Parfitt not bringing help?"

She nodded at Adam to follow and headed toward Alfie Aubry's trailer. "Remember when I asked him why he didn't find that woman out in the field? He said something about not doing a 'grid search'. How's a guy who writes cooking tips know what a grid search is?"

"How do *you* know what it is?"

"I dealt with my share of police cases back in Boston."

"Maybe he saw it on a rerun of *CSI*. Is it that big a thing?"

"It's not just me. Something about that guy bothered Alfie early on."

"How do you know?"

"Remember this morning, you two were watching Alfie from my house, it looked like he was taking down your plate numbers."

"Yeah, he was going to contact Motor Vehicle, try to find out who I am."

"Right, ok, but why'd he take down *Parfitt's* numbers? Something wasn't sitting right with Alfie about him. Think back; remember him checking out Parfitt's plates?"

They were at Aubry's trailer now, standing where Carl had left Adam's dead Bronco.

"I didn't think much about it then…" Adam mused. She could see him trying to make sense of it, but it wasn't coming together for him, much like it hadn't come together for her…until now.

"Look at the mud on your car, Adam."

"Ok, that's how we figured it'd been on one of these access roads, probably the one to my old house."

Liz took a moment, partly because she wanted to be sure of where she was going with this…and partly because she didn't like where her thinking was going. "Want to explain to me how on that muddy road, this mess all around your car…how your plates manage to be squeaky clean?"

Adam's face went cold. "I never noticed…"

"I want you to think back to this morning, again, when you two were watching Alfie. Alfie walked over to Parfitt's car…and what did he do?"

Adam frowned. "It looked like he was taking down Parfitt's plate numbers."

"Before that."

"Before…?"

"Remember him squatting down…"

Now Adam's face went slack. "He had to clean the plate off to read it."

"But Parfitt's car was clean; he'd just come off the 201. It didn't hit me until I watched him pull out just now. His car was all muddy from going up and down these back roads, and then I remembered Alfie cleaning off the plates this morning when he shouldn't have had to. How come his plate – and *only* his plate – was so muddy Alfie had to clean it off to read it?"

Adam ran it over and over in his head. Liz could see he kept coming up with the same answer she had, but he'd shake it off. *He's saying; That can't be, because he doesn't want it to be.*

"Why'd Alfie have to do that, Adam?" she pushed.

"He switched plates? Why?"

"Whatever the reason, Parfitt didn't want Alfie to figure it out. Or anybody else for that matter. When I was examining Alfie's body, I found his notebook. It looks like the pages with the plate numbers had been torn out."

She nodded at Adam to follow her, again, as she headed toward her house. "We've been assuming you were stripped of every bit of identification so you wouldn't know who you were when you came to."

"And I didn't. I *still* --"

"Except that doesn't make sense."

"How does it not --"

"Because whoever took all your identification would have no way of knowing you'd have amnesia when you woke up. For all they knew, you'd wake up knowing exactly who you were, you'd know people you could call to prove it."

Adam stopped; Liz stopped with him. They were standing on the shoulder of the 201. Adam looked up and down the empty highway as if there was an answer to see somewhere on that road. He shook his head. "It-*doesn't*-make-sense!"

He wasn't just confused; Liz could see he was *pained*. The whole day had already made no sense to him and now people were dead; she couldn't imagine how much more of a torture it was to throw this on top of it. He stopped looking up and down the road, turned to Liz; *Please help me* plain on his face.

"It wasn't so *you* wouldn't know who you were," Liz said. "It was so *we* wouldn't know."

Which didn't seem to clear anything up for Adam.

"Stranger shows up in a strange town," Liz went on. "Wrecked car, injured, blood in the car that doesn't belong to him, babbling about some missing woman... You were going to have to prove to *us* you weren't some bad guy involved in something nasty. And maybe in the process, you'd lead whoever is behind this --"

"Parfitt?"

She gave a resigned shrug. "Looks like. In the process, you might lead him to…to…"

"To what?"

"To whatever it was you and that poor woman came up here for. That's *got* to be what this is all about because that's the only way all this shit makes any kind of sense. Sort of. I think." She shrugged again; this was as good as her thinking on the matter was going to get and going by Adam's weak agreeing shake of the head, he concurred to the same degree.

Liz started across the empty highway to her house. Adam followed. She stopped at her house, sat on the front steps. Adam stood off from her, puzzled at the halt.

"What's the matter?"

"I want to try something, Adam."

"Ok."

"The only help our probably-not-a-journalist friend is going for is help for him. I think the clock is running for us."

"How much time do you think we have?"

"He had at least a good half-hour in front of him before he could call out of the area for help. The woman in the field, Dinsmore, she was with the Portland police, so I'm assuming this business traces back to Portland and that's where he'll call for help. It's going to be a couple of hours for whoever he calls to get up here. We need to know what this is all about before they get here."

"What is it you want to try?"

She fixed him with a hard stare. "Do you trust me?"

He blinked, surprised at the question. "Sure!"

"Don't 'sure' me, mister! Less than an hour ago you were thinking I'd killed my friend. Parfitt put that bug in your ear, didn't he?"

Adam flushed, looked away. "Look, I'm sorry about that. It's only because I don't know what's going on. I don't know who any of you people are --"

"You're sounding like Parfitt, Adam, so just give me a straight answer: do you trust me?"

Adam pulled himself erect, returned her hard stare with one of his own: "Yes."

"Good, because I'm going to have to trust you, too."

"How so?"

"What I want to try violates a bucketload of professional ethics, medical protocols, and for what I'm going to be doing, is also illegal. If you ever open your yap about this, I could have my license suspended, maybe even revoked. So, my second question is: can I trust *you*?"

This time, no hesitation: "Yes, Liz."

She nodded, stood, brushed the flaking stoop paint off the seat of her pants. "Let's do it," and she nodded Adam inside.

She stood at the bottom of the stairs for a moment after he went in, looked up at the darkening sky trying to decide if what she was going to do was insane or just stupid.

From Carl's church not far up the road from her house, it was Hall & Oates:

Some things are better left unsaid
Some strings are better left undone
Some hearts are better left unbroken
That, Carl, Liz mused, is the problem…

Chapter Nine

Adam had been waiting for her in the front room/office. "You ok?"

She nodded. "Go into my bedroom, pull the shades, make yourself comfortable on the bed."

Adam's eyebrows wig-wagged and he put on a cartoonish smirk. "Goodness, Doctor, we hardly know each other! But if you insist…"

"If you didn't already have a dent in your head, I'd slap you. This is purely professional, now get in there."

When she came into the darkened bedroom, pushing a utility table and pulling her wheeled medical stool, she found Adam in a mock-*Playboy* pose on her bed: on his side, legs curled around each other, head propped on one hand, and the kind of overdone seductive look worthy of a Bugs Bunny cartoon.

"It's going to be ironic if, when you get your memory back, we find you have absolutely no sense of humor."

But the site of the table and stool had already drained the mirth from Adam. He nodded at the hardware on the table. "That certainly kills the mood."

"Want some soft music?"

"Not sure that would help."

"Get comfy." As Adam arranged the bed's pillows so he was in a half-reclining position, Liz turned on the night table lamp, brought the table and stool close to the bed, then took her seat.

As soon as Adam had set himself into the pillows, his eyes went to the stainless steel instrument tray on the table, partly in curiosity, partly already wincing at what might be coming his way.

Liz wasn't surprised; he had reason. On the tray was a length of thin rubber tubing, a bottle of isopropyl alcohol, a jar of cotton balls, a Band-Aid, a hypodermic syringe, and a small vial filled with a clear fluid.

"Can you do anything about this wave of apprehension I'm feeling?" Adam said.

"Scaredy cat. Ok, well, the thing is I didn't specialize in psychiatry or neurology, so I'm working more on slightly informed guesswork than expertise.

Adam winced, again, more sharply this time. "*Slightly* informed? 'Slightly' is not exactly comforting."

Liz laughed, nodding; she could see his point. "In my inexpert view, it strikes me you've been trying to force yourself to remember, and maybe it's like, oh, I don't know, maybe it's like constipation; trying to force it is only going to give you a headache."

"Or the mental equivalent of a hemorrhoid."

"If you want to torture the analogy, yeah."

Adam nodded at the small vial. "And I'm guessing you want to give me the psychological equivalent of an enema to induce the psychological equivalent of diarrhea."

Now it was Liz's turn to wince. "I am really sorry I ever used that analogy…but yeah. This," and she held up the vial, "is pentothal."

"Isn't that the stuff you see in the old war movies? The Nazis are interrogating some poor slob and they give him truth serum to get him to talk? 'Ve haf vays of making you talk, American *schweinhund*'."

"Whatever you were in your previous life, you weren't an actor. The movies are the movies. Pentothal isn't really a truth serum, it just lowers your inhibitions, like having a couple of drinks. Well, maybe quite a few drinks. But it's not reliable and that's why it's illegal for the police to use it. Sometimes you get the truth. Sometimes you just get what someone *thinks* is the truth. Sometimes you get what someone *wants* the truth to be. And sometimes you get pure bullshit because that's how the human mind works. But maybe, possibly, hopefully, this could loosen up your memory block and we just might get some answers. Maybe. Possibly. Hope-"

"I get it," Adam cut her off, then a curious frown: "What're *you* doing with pentothal?"

"It's actually a mild anesthetic. Jocko slips and opens up his finger with a carving knife, I'll give him a little of this while I sew him up. That kind of thing."

"Is it dangerous?"

"Physically, no, not at the dosage I'll be using."

Adam held up a finger: "Something about the way you said 'physically'…"

Liz squirmed in her seat, hesitated.

"C'mon, Liz, out with it."

With a resigned sigh, "Typically, people who've been under don't remember a lot of what they said while they were under. Sometimes they don't remember *any* of it." She reached into the pocket of her jacket, pulled out a small Sony voice recorder and set it on the utility table. "I was going to record the session, for reference later, even though I'd have to destroy the recording at some point."

"Because if anybody got a hold of it, you could wind up selling shoes."

She nodded. "Yup."

"But this way, even if I forgot everything, I could play it back and --"

"And that's the question."

"You're going to have to explain that."

She fidgeted with the voice recorder, pushing it this way and that on the table. "See, Adam, we're not going to have any control over what you remember, providing you remember anything. It's possible you might recall things…things you wish had stayed forgotten." She gave Adam a moment to let that percolate. "I debated with myself whether or not to even tell you about this," and she tapped the recorder. "But then I figured it should be up to you."

Adam held up his left arm. Liz couldn't tell if that hard studying look was aimed at the scars on his wrist or the finger where a ring had once sat. He lowered his arm, turned to look at the afternoon's orange glow around the drawn shades. "Getting late in the day," he said quietly. He took a deep breath, let it out slowly. "Do it. Record it. "

"You're sure?"

He nodded. "Two people are dead, Liz, and it has something to do with me. Don't you think I owe it to them?"

"This isn't about what *I* think, Adam --"

"Do it."

Still, she hesitated, waiting for some last second rethinking, but his firm look at her never wavered. She nodded, took the rubber tubing and tied it tightly around his upper arm to get a vein to rise. Once she got a vein, she soaked one of the cotton balls with alcohol and swabbed a target area. She took up the syringe and drew 50 milligrams from the vial. "Ready?"

Adam nodded and looked away.

"Still a wuss," which made him smile until the needle bit. When the injection was completed, she untied the tubing, put another cotton ball over the small spot of blood and held it in place with the Band-Aid. "I gave you a light dose, enough to put you into a twilight state; not quite totally asleep, not quite awake."

"How long does it take to work?"

"Not long. Just lay back, close your eyes, relax." She turned off the night table lamp, switched on the voice recorder. It only took a minute or so before his breathing became slow and easy.

Ok, Adam, here we go…

Liz wasn't sure how to start, so she went with the obvious: "Adam, can you hear me?"

A muffled grunt in response.

"Adam?"

"No' my name." The words came out slurred, as if his lips were numb.

"What is your name?"

Adam's face took on some vague wrinkles. A frown, Liz guessed. "It's… Can't quite…"

"That's ok. Can I call you Adam?"

"Sure."

Now what? They didn't have a class in interrogation techniques in med school. After a moment's consideration, Liz went with, "Adam, the woman who drove up here with you, Sergeant Dinsmore --"

"Didn' know her name."

"Then how did you know her? Did you know her?"

That vague frown, again, but before it was concentration. This time, it was the effort to get things right: "Yes. No." Adam shook his head, frustrated. "Walked by my shop ever' day. Got to recognize her. Wave hello. Said 's on her way to work."

"So, you talked to her."

"Came in one day."

"To your shop."

A sleepy affirmative nod.

"What kind of shop was it, Adam?"

Again, face wrinkling in concentration. Still sounding unsure: "Collected…things."

"Collected things? What kind of things."

"Old things."

"Was this an antique store?"

She could see the struggle on his face; she thought even if he'd been fully conscious, this was something he wouldn't be able to quite explain.

"Some. Just…old things. Things I liked. Estates. Auctions. Someone come in, need money… Things I liked. Said I was buried in a cemetery…other people's memories."

"Who said that?"

"Woman."

"The woman who drove to Warsaw with you."

A nod.

"Did you know she was with the police?"

"Not then."

"So, she came in one day."

"Said she's curious. Couldn' make sense…"

"Make sense of what?"

"Things. Some had value. Some…junk. She…" Suddenly, Adam's face began to twist in a new way, not in a sleepy or vague way, but with the clarity of some deep pain.

"She what? What did she do? What's the matter, Adam?"

"Ask me…ask me…wha' my wife thought…all this stuff. My *wife*… Told her no wife," and now his chest began to heave with sobs so deep Liz wondered if they might drive him to full consciousness.

She didn't think about it; it was almost instinctive – to take his near hand between hers. He might've been in a somnambulant state, but he squeezed her hand so hard Liz came close to gasping in pain.

"Did she leave you, Adam? Your wife?"

"Dead. Both of them."

My God… and she instantly regretted, in the most self-punishing kind of way, putting Adam through this. "Both? What do you mean 'both'?"

"Nikki – Nicole – and li'l Gigi *Oh God…*"

"GeeGee was your daughter?" Liz guessed.

"Gloria-Gail. We called her Gigi. Little Gigi. Both of them…"

Liz felt helpless. She'd sat at the bedside of the dying, sat with the families of the dying, and felt the same way; that any token action, anything said would only feel terribly lame. *No point,* Ellis used to tell her. *There's nothing you can do.* And she would agree, but say, *I know that…but I'd rather do a useless something than nothing.* She slipped one hand free and set it on Adam's chest, stroking it lightly. "It's ok, Adam. I'm here."

This explained the scars on his wrist, the missing ring. But the scars were old; this couldn't possibly be connected to what was going on now. Still, she knew she had to let him go on; she had to be sure.

The stroking seemed to calm him down, at least for the moment, not completely but to the point where the sobs stopped and he talked in what seemed like one, long, endless sigh. "Work for a bank. Promotion. Big man, big shot. Never home. Didn' see her grow up. Always away. Thought, take 'em to France. Thanks for putting up wi' me. I 's always traveling, they'd never been anywhere. Never been on a plane. Never been out of New England."

His face smoothed; his lips turned in a smile melancholy with the memory. "Shoulda seen their faces… Flying in, they could see Eiffel Tower… Their faces. Little Gigi…all eyes. Worth it jus' to see that look. Firs' day, take 'em to lunch, café on the street. Like the movies. Ready to leave, phone… 'Don't take it, Daddy, we're on vacation.' 'Sweets, that's what pays for this. You and mommy go. I'll catch up'." His face twisted in pain, again. "Oh, Christ…*Oh, Christ!*"

"What happened?"

"Bomb. Terrorist, they said. Never found out who. Had to identify… Oh, God, Nikki, Gigi… "The sobs came back, more violently than before. "Couldn't even recognize…Jesus, Jesus, *Jesus… I sent them!*"

She looked over at the voice recorder, tempted, for the moment, not just to turn it off, but bat it away, smash it. *What've you done, Liz? What'd you do to this guy?* She felt her own eyes stinging, as much in pain over what she was putting Adam through as in sympathy for the man's deep hurt. "Take it easy, Adam," she said, aware her own voice was trembling. "Let's not talk about that, ok? Let's focus on yesterday." *Yeah, c'mon, Liz, focus on yesterday. That's going to be the only thing that makes this poor man's anguish worth it.* "Adam, this shop of yours –
"

"Came home. Quit job…damn job. Sold house, couldn' live there anymore. Sold everything. Start the shop. Buried myself in old things. Other people's memories. Good things." The sobbing eased, and Adam seemed to sink into a numbed sadness, his hand in her hand eased its grip, but still held on.

The shop, Liz. Work the shop. "Who, Adam? Who started the shop? Your name. Your name must've been somewhere, on a piece of paper, a name plate. Think! Can you see it?"

His brows drew together, like he was squinting at something in the distance. "Mmm, yeahhhh…Can see it. Front window. Proprietor."

"Who's the proprietor, Adam?"

"Pratt. C. Pratt. Cyril."

"Cyril Pratt? Is that you?"

A smile; a real smile. "God, name's awful. Always hated that. Cy. Made people call me Cy. Cyril; Jesus."

"Ok, Cy. The woman who came in your shop. Sergeant Dinsmore. You didn't know she was with the police. One day, she comes in."

"Yes'erday."

"She came into the shop yesterday? Why? Just to look around?"

He shook his head. "Came in, gimme a box, li'l box. Trinket box. Said hold it, don' open. Not back in three days, sell it."

"Was she pawning it?"

"Didn' ask f' money. Jus' said hold it."

"Was it valuable? Could you tell?"

Adam's nose wrinkled. "Junk. Kid stuff. Like for a li'l girl. She came back. Tha' nigh'. Had closed up, doing the books, someone banging on the door. Let her in."

"Why did she come back?"

"Said they knew." Adam's face went cold; fear.

"Who knew? Who was 'they'? Did she say?"

A shake of his head. "Said my life…in danger. Sorry got me in. Had to get me out of town. Could see she was hurt. Didn' know how bad, I swear, didn' know she, she…" The pained look, again.

She squeezed his hand. "It's ok, Adam, um, Cy. I know you didn't know. It wasn't your fault."

"I said hospital, take you to the… She said I take her to…hospital, they find her…she's dead. Said, get the box. Have a car? They know mine. She drove." He gave a wry little smile. "Said I'd stop for red lights. Had to get out fast."

"Why did you come here? Why Warsaw?"

"She said they know every place I know. Need a place they don't know. A place only *I* knew."

"So, you came here where you used to live."

"Had to hide box."

Ok, this is it; we're <u>there</u>. "Where did you hide it, Adam? At your old house?"

"Hidden." A bit of a satisfied smile. "Nobody knows but me."

"She never told you why the box was important?"

Another shake of the head. That inner pain rolled back in. "Driving away, could see she was… I didn' know."

"I know you didn't, Cy."

"She…She passed out…" A great, long sigh. "'S all. Don' 'member anything after…" Then another sigh, and in a hissed stream of self-hatred, *"I…sent…them…"*

He seemed to unwind, then, not so much exhausted as empty. She gently let his hand go, turned off the voice recorder, left the room and came back with a damp cloth. She softly wiped away the sweat which had built up on his forehead, the tears still wet on his cheeks.

"Cy, listen to me. Relax. Let yourself fall asleep. Go ahead, Cy: sleep."

And in a bit, as she dabbed at his face with the cloth, he did.

Liz stood away from the bed, looked at the figure sunk into her sagging mattress, feeling as mentally exhausted as Adam no doubt did, drained as much by guilt as by sympathy.

Have a good sleep, Cy. You earned it.

Evening

Chapter Ten

Liz was sitting at her desk in the front office, poking her way through a plate of scrambled eggs with so little enthusiasm they were growing cold even as she ate them, when she heard Cy *nee* Adam shuffle in.

He still looked like he was shaking off the effects of the pentothal which concerned Liz since there weren't supposed to be any aftereffects. But then she saw the voice recorder in his hand and knew his groggy state had more to do with digesting what he'd heard than the drug. He squinted out the windows, looked surprised at the darkness.

"Jesus, how long have I been out?"

"Just a few hours. I thought you could use the sleep."

He nodded a thanks and she pointed to the chair on the other side of the desk. "Are you hungry, Cy?"

He winced. "'Cyril.' What was my mom thinking? When I get around to remembering if she's still alive, if she is, she and I are going to have a long talk about that. I've gotten kind of used to Adam. Why don't we stay with that. Call it a nickname."

Liz chuckled. "Good, because 'Cyril' --"

"Cy."

"Even 'Cy' was going to be an adjustment after a day of 'Adam'. Ok, Adam, I was saying, I got a little hungry, scrambled up some eggs. There's more in the pan. I could heat them up, no problem."

Adam shook his head. "Do you have coffee? Just coffee, then."

Liz went to the cramped kitchenette opposite her bedroom, poured him a mug from the Mr. Coffee on the little counter. "How do you take it?"

"Black," he called back.

She came back, set the mug down by him, went back to her seat. "You remembered that? That you take your coffee black?"

He smiled. "What I remember is that I prefer tea, but I think I need the coffee." He sat quietly for a bit; a chill ran through him.

"The temperature does drop a bit at night," Liz said, "and this place isn't great on heat."

He nodded, cupping his hands around the warm mug. He stared down into the black liquid for a long, silent time, then looked over at the voice recorder he'd set on the table. "I played it."

"I'm sorry about -- ... Well, you know. I wasn't sure I should've left it for you."

"I needed to hear it. All of it."

She nodded but she wasn't as sure as he was. What a choice: an empty hole where your life had been or recalling that kind of horror. "Has everything come back to you?"

He cocked his head. "Some of it. A lot of it. The parts that hurt the most. I guess *because* they hurt the most. There's still missing pieces, but I've got answers to a lot of questions now."

"That's good. But now we have a new question."

"Which is?"

"Which is, what do we do now?"

He took a long, contemplative breath, then a sip of the coffee, made a sour face.

"Sorry," Liz said, "but domestic qualities are not my forte."

Adam forced another sip with the same face-souring results. "Well, as unpalatable as this is, first thing is I'm going to finish this coffee because, unpalatable as it is, I think I need it. And after I'm done choking this goop down, I'm going to ask you to drive us out to my old house."

The yellow moon was highly luminescent, a strangely glowing lantern almost bright enough that Liz could've driven without her headlights, washing the open ground around Warsaw in a pale, color-draining light. Still, she drove cautiously, remembering a patient two years ago she'd had to rush down to Northern Light Hospital because he'd gone through his windshield after hitting a moose which had suddenly appeared in the middle of the road one night.

When she turned onto the access road, she was even more careful, not doing the rocketing that had so terrified Adam earlier that day. It was night; things came out of the woods at night and were often too frightened or too dumb to get out of the way.

"I was thinking…" Adam mused.

"Good for you. I like thinking. Keeps the brain from going flabby."

"You thought Parfitt was up to something because of that 'grid search' remark."

"It was one of the things."

"But you seem to know a lot about police work yourself. I mean, I saw the way you examined that woman in the field, then your friend…"

"Are we back to you thinking I had something to do with Alfie's --"

"No no no! That's not what I meant! I was just curious about how you know so much."

It was, Liz thought, a certain flavor of sad that she did know so much. "You work in any big city hospital, even in the nicest city, and sooner or later you'll see all the kinds of mayhem people do to each other…and themselves: gunshot wounds, stab wounds, beatings, abused spouses – either sex – child abuse, sexual assaults, some of them so -- … You wonder what puts stuff like that in a person's head. Drug OD's, some bizarre and grotesque accidents, suicide attempts --"

It was out of her mouth before she could think better of it, one of those things for which she wished there was a rewind button. Out of the corner of her eye, she could see Adam, in the glow of the dashboard lights, looking at his right wrist. Trying to find a positive way out, she said, "You were lucky."

"Lucky?"

"Someone found you."

"What makes you think someone found me?"

"When we'd see, well, somebody try it the way you did, often we'd see what're called 'hesitation cuts'; shallow cuts because they're working up the nerve to making the big one. Unless yours was so shallow that they completely healed without leaving a mark, you didn't hesitate. I'm talking to you today because someone found you before, well, you know…"

"No one found me."

Adam let that hang in the air for a moment. Liz flashed a quick look to Adam. In the greenish dash lights, she could see he hadn't gone quiet; he was working up the nerve to go further. Then…

"I chickened out. You're right; I didn't hesitate. I sat in my bathtub, I cut my wrists, and as soon as I started bleeding, I realized…I didn't want to die."

She gave him another quick look; he was ashamed.

"You shouldn't feel bad about that. I'm sure your wife wouldn't have wanted you --"

"Yeah, yeah, I know, they would've wanted me to --" in a mock grand tone, " – live on! And that's how I rationalized it, how I've kept rationalizing it. They would've wanted me to live my life, to move on, to blah blah blah."

And now she understood. "So, you couldn't do it that way, but you stopped living. You buried yourself in that shop of yours."

"I hadn't thought of it that way, but yeah, I guess. I surrounded myself with old things, things from better times."

"A cemetery of other people's memories."

"That were certainly better than mine."

"When was this?"

"Soon after I came back from France. I brought them back, buried them, went home and… That was about five years ago."

Liz felt a twinge. "Funny. That's about the time I moved up here." *Maybe I was trying to bury myself someplace safe, too.*

They were at the house. Liz turned her wagon in to face the house, left the engine running and the headlights on. She reached into the glove compartment where she kept a heavy Maglite. "Ready?"

Adam's head was bowed; she knew he was still musing over it all – why he'd wanted to die, then not wanting to die, then not living in his shop filled with the remnants of other people's lives.

"Adam?"

"See, the thing I can't shake, that I'll never be able to shake…" Something that was a cross between a sigh and a sob. *"I-sent-them."*

She could see he was on the verge of sliding into a tunnel of grief. She put a hand firmly on his forearm. "Adam, let's do this," she said with a firmness to match her grip.

Adam shook the mood off, nodded, and they climbed out of the car. Liz started walking toward the house, heard Adam's footsteps stop. She turned. "What's the matter?"

He nodded: nothing. He pointed toward the sky. The black dome was heavily starred, as if God had taken a handful of bits of light the way one would take a handful of sand and tossed them into the firmament.

"I'd forgotten…" he said, his voice soft, awed. "I'd forgotten how many there were." His right hand came up, the fingers moving as if he was trying to grab hold of something and she saw in his face that he was; he was trying to pull up another memory. "After my father died, where did we go? We moved…to Portland. Yes, my mother had family there. And I remember…I remember, I think it was our first night…I saw there were so few stars. She explained to me how the city lights wash them out. And I was sad, so sad… I'd lost my dad, my home, and even this…" and he pointed back up to the bejeweled night.

"I envy you."

He seemed genuinely puzzled. "How so?"

It was her turn to point skyward. "It was like I said this afternoon: you grow up in a place like this and you take it for granted. You don't realize what a gift it is."

He took another moment gazing upward, soaking it in, basking in it, relishing it, and then with a deep, firming breath, pointed toward the house. "Let's do this."

She stopped just outside the front door. "*HEY!*" she yelled and banged on the wall.

"What the hell was that for?"

"In case anything is living in there."

"Oh," Adam said, obviously agreeing that this was a good idea.

She had the Maglite, so she led the way. Her car's headlights made two brilliant squares of light on the far wall of the front room as they beamed through the front windows, but beyond that, the corners fell into shadow, and the rear of the house was completely dark. Liz swept the Maglite this way and that, looking for…for what? "I hate to point out the obvious, Adam, but you went through this place today and came up with nothing."

"That's because I was going through it as an adult with no memory. Now I'm going through it as a kid who does remember. This way." He walked directly toward a small room on a rear corner of the house. "This was my bedroom."

Like the rest of the house, it was, naturally, empty except for water stains on the walls from the leaky roof, papery dried leaves which had blown in through the broken window.

Liz kept the light on Adam as he went to the far wall. "My bed was right around here…" He began testing floorboards with one foot, then, "This one." He dropped to his knees. "Do you have something I can pry this up with?"

Liz handed him her keychain. "There's a penknife on that."

He popped the little blade out and began working the floorboard loose. "This was my secret stash. I kept my comic books in here, my favorite toys, candy I would sneak out at night after they went to sleep. Mounds were my favorite."

Liz smiled. "Mine was Almond Joy."

"Aren't they always side by side on the store shelf?"

"Not always. But mostly."

He stopped working the floorboard, and for the first time since she'd bandaged his head that morning, Liz saw him smile without inhibition, without some undertone of melancholy or shade of guilt about finding a good moment. She found herself sending the same smile back.

He went back to the board and popped it free. He started to reach into the black space under the floor when Liz stomped heavily on the floor. He looked at her quizzically, but then understood: "In case something's living there."

She grinned and nodded.

Perhaps that in mind is why he reached into the dark space more tentatively. Then his eyes grew wide. "Jesus, what's that?"

"What is it?"

Something pulled at Adam, pulled him down flat on the floor.

"Adam!"

He pulled himself up laughing.

"You shit!" she spat out, not sure if she wanted to laugh or bring the Maglite down on his grinning head. "I guess you remembered something else; that you have a dick's sense of humor."

"Evidently." He had his arm out now and in his hand was a small silver box, almost glowing in the beam of her light. It was small enough to fit in one hand, had a curved lid and was decorated with raised curlicues.

She was no expert, but she could easily see Adam had been right; this was no artifact of value. It was silver paint, not silver, and it was flaking off in a number of places, lightweight, too, made of something cheap, like tin. It was the kind of thing a little girl would keep her plastic play jewelry in, maybe the few dollars she would get in a birthday card, maybe any little thing a small girl would think, the way kids do, was of value.

Liz remembered the photos of the young Dinsmore woman, and it made sense; this was something she'd had as a little girl, that she'd held onto into her adulthood, that she'd brought into her marriage with her because the value was not in the object but with the childhood attached to it.

"Well," Liz said.

"Well." Adam undid the little hook holding the lid closed, pulled the lid up.

"Well *crap!*"

The blue felt-lined interior of the box was empty.

Liz began stalking angrily around the room. "Jesus Christ, all this, all this *shit* we've been through, and for nothing?"

"Bring that light over here, Liz. Look; this isn't right." He was pointing to the felt lining on the lid. It wasn't glued along the curve of the lid, but straight across its bottom. "It shouldn't be like this. Here, you can see how sloppy this is glued. This wasn't done at the factory." He picked up the keychain and pen knife from where he'd left them on the floor and used the knife blade to cut the lid's lining away. Tucked inside the little space, folded into a small square, was a piece of paper. Adam set the box down and began unfolding the paper.

There was a letterhead – CHAMPAGNE – with the same design that had been on the matchbook Adam had been carrying that morning. Handwritten in pen on the paper were two columns, one of ten names, the other of figures ranging from 250 to 100. Some of the names had "Sgt" in front of them, others led with "PO."

At the top of the name column was "Sgt Parfitt." His was the only name with a "300" across from it in the numbers column.

Adam was shaking his head, still unable to make sense of it, but it was clear to Liz: "They're cops," she said. "'PO' stands for 'police officer' – patrolmen."

"What're these numbers?"

"Bribes, Adam. That's what they're getting paid each week."

"Parfitt --"

"He gets the most. He must be the top guy. What's with this 'Champagne' on the letterhead?"

"I remember now. She told me – the dead woman – it was a hangout for some of the policemen at her station. These cops, I guess. The matches I had; they were hers. She gave them to me to light a cigarette for her while she was driving."

"Now we know what someone thought was worth killing for. And why Dinsmore thought they'd kill you or anybody else who had this."

"Your friend the constable?"

"My guess is Parfitt knew that once Alfie ran down those license plates, he'd start figuring out Parfitt wasn't who he said he was. Then he cut the phone lines to make sure nobody else could figure it out either. We should get back to town and figure out what to do."

Adam nodded, tucked the paper in his jacket pocket and started to get up.

"Adam, don't forget the box. Her husband's going to want it."

Chapter Eleven

Morahan's had officially closed about the time the sun had gone down; there had never been much of a dinner crowd for the place. The neon "Open" sign had been switched off, the lights along the front windows as well. Liz and Adam sat at a table with Jocko Morahan and his wife, staring out the front windows, watching evening turn to full on night. They'd been strategizing without much success.

"Where's he going to go?" Liz said when Jocko had suggested Adam light out of town. "If he goes south and they catch him on the road, well, that's it."

"He could head north, for the border."

Liz shook her head. "These are cops, Jocko. If they haven't already, they'll put out a statewide APB for him, some bullshit story about why he's wanted, maybe even an 'armed and dangerous' warning hoping somebody gets nervous and -- … "She cut herself off, reprimanding herself for momentarily forgetting the potential dead man was sitting next to her. "Point is," she sighed, "there's no safe place for him to run."

"Doesn't matter. I'm not running."

Liz turned to Adam. His voice had been quiet, but steady. Firm. His eyes were fixed on the tabletop with its years of scratches and nicks and a carved initial or two.

"Listen, mister," Morahan said, "you don't know how many's comin', what kind of artillery they're bringin' --"

"I'm not running." Adam pointed at the Purdeys mounted over the bar. "Can I borrow one of those?"

"Seriously?"

Adam nodded, although Liz saw it less as a firm commitment then a grim resignation. "Seriously."

Morahan didn't move. He looked from Adam to Liz, then from Liz to his wife.

"You heard the man," Violet said and gave Jocko something that was a cross between a shove and a punch to the arm.

Not looking too cheery at the prospect, Morahan pulled himself heavily from his chair, went behind the bar, kicked a footstool over so he could step up and lift one of the shotguns from its perch. "Do you even know how to use one of these?"

"I've never fired any kind of gun in my life."

"Great." Morahan reached under the bar and came up with a box of 12 gauge shells, brought gun and ammo back to the table. "You sure about this?"

Adam took a deep breath like he was mulling it over. He looked at Liz with an odd little smile. "No."

"Great. Ok, quick lesson: this opens the breach. You drop your shells in like this, and after you shoot, you open 'er up again and she'll pop the empties out. When you shoot, tuck 'er tight in your shoulder like this 'cause she bucks like a wild horse. You don't and your shot'll go wild and you might even bust your own nose. Aim here --" and his hand circled the middle of his torso, " -- so you're bound to hit somethin' with some of the shot. A rookie like you, anything past thirty yards – say from here to the middle of the highway – I'd say don't bother." He handed the gun to Adam. "Ok, you do it. Look, I don't wanna sound petty or nothin', but you're not plannin' on usin' my place as your Alamo, are ya? It may not be much, but it's all I got."

"That's flatterin' as hell to me, Jocko, thanks," Violet said.

"You know what I mean, Vi."

Liz had made her decision as soon as Adam had called for the Purdey. "My place. Besides, these big windows won't inhibit flying bullets very well. But somebody should go for help. You, Jocko, why don't you take Violet, head north, away from them, and when you get to the border, have the border cops call the staties."

Morahan's face wrinkled as he did some considering. Then he nodded toward his wife. "Vi should go."

Violet's eyes popped a bit. "What?"

"Go in the van," Jocko said, "They won't be lookin' for somebody like you in the delivery van."

"And what're you gonna do? You think you're Bruce Willis or somethin'?"

"Nothin'. I'm gonna just sit here in the dark with that other Purdey and not do nothin' less one of these clowns tries to get in."

"Jocko, this isn't your fight," Adam said.

"They come through that front door, and it is."

Liz and Adam looked to Violet, but she just shrugged. "Trust me: there's no talking to him once he gets like this. I just don't know why he never gets like this with a *good* idea."

It was an ancient Ford box van, "Morahan's" painted along each side over some pretty bad, barely recognizable renderings of some kinds of sandwiches, done by a dope-smoking drop-out from the Art program at the University of Maine-Presque Isle. The windshield was dotted with bug splatters, every wheel well enlarged by body rot.

Morahan walked his wife to where the van was parked out back of his place, held the door open for her.

"Shouldn't be a problem you goin' north 'cause Doc says they're comin' up from Portland. You might even get to the border 'fore they get here. Then, like the doc says, tell 'em what's goin' on and have 'em call the troopers in."

Violet started to step up into the van, then stopped and turned to her husband. "You should come with me. They won't be lookin' for some broken down ol' couple neither."

"Who's broken down?" He forced a smile. "I'm gonna be fine, Vi. It's a just-in-case kinda thing. They'll be after that guy in there and they'll be over at the doc's house."

"You're not bein' smart, Jocko."

"When'd you ever know me to do somethin' smart?"

"Well, you did marry me."

"That's true. Um, look, uh, Vi…be careful. Try and keep it 'tween the lines, ok? You know how the steerin' wobbles. And watch out who's crossin' the road at night. You 'member the doc, last year, had to take Vern Ziffel down to Northern Light 'cause him hittin' that moose. And I know you need to rush, but you know she won't take bein' pushed too hard. Won't be doin' us much good you blow the engine. 'Sides, we can't afford a new van."

"Nice you got your priorities."

And then Jocko did something he hadn't done in so long he couldn't remember the last time; he took his wife in his arms and held her close and was surprised at how tightly her arms closed around him. "I'm gonna see you in a couple hours," he said quietly, his cheek burrowing deep into the wiry nest of her hair.

"Don't do anything else dumb, ok?" she mumbled into his shoulder.

"You know me, Vi."

"That's what I'm afraid of."

Then he gently pushed her away and held her hand as she climbed up and slid behind the wheel. The van's engine didn't turn over at first, and for a moment Jocko wondered if she'd be leaving at all, then with a cough and a couple of puffs of oily black smoke from the exhaust, the engine caught, ran at a rough idle until Violet expertly fed it a bit more gas, and a bit more until it ran more or less smoothly if noisily. Only then did Jocko close the door, they exchanged small little smiles as goodbyes before the van rumbled and bounced across the open ground – "The lights, Vi, the lights!" – and the headlights came on as Violet found her way to the highway.

Jocko watched until the van's one good taillight disappeared into the dark.

It was deeply night, now, the sky a velvety black heavily bejeweled with diamond points of light, the countryside laid out pale but clear under the yellow moon. Even though Carl's church was strangely silent, the night was noisy with loud choruses of *chirrups* from the tall grass and the dark within the copses of trees along the highway.

They were walking across the 201 from Morahan's toward Liz's place. She watched Adam fumble with the shotgun, trying to find some natural fit for it in his hands and never finding it. It brought to Liz's mind something she'd read in a movie review years ago, a comment about an actor who obviously didn't smoke trying to pretend he did. The reviewer wrote the actor made the attempts "…with all the grace of a man falling out of a tree." To her, that was Adam fiddling with the Purdey.

He stopped in the middle of the highway, looked up at the glitter in the dark sky. This wasn't like when they'd been out at his old homestead, enjoying a reminiscence. Even under the pale light of the moon, Liz could see it in Adam's face, the look of a man appreciating – savoring -- something he might never see again. Then his shoulders rose and fell in a silent sigh, and they continued on to her house.

He stopped, again, his head cocked toward the gentle racket coming to them from out of the dark. "Boy, that's something I didn't remember."

"What?"

"How loud the damned crickets are out here!"

She laughed quietly, happy there was something to laugh about. They continued on to her house. "My first night up here, I thought they were some kind of bird, thought they had to be. Maybe they're just bigger than Massachusetts crickets."

"Sound like maneaters."

She laughed again.

At the house, she paused on the front steps, pointed south down the highway. "We should park ourselves here for now. Better view down the highway. We'll see them in plenty of time."

They sat together on the top step.

From the stairs, they could see Jocko toddling first over to Cargill's where he spent a minute with the storekeeper, then heading toward a little cluster of houses further up the road.

"What's he doing?" Adam asked.

"I told Jocko to tell people in this part of town to lay low, stay dark."

Adam nodded, agreeing it was a sane idea.

"You want some coffee?" she asked. "Oh, that's right; you prefer tea. I think I have some. "

It looked like he wanted to say something, held it back.

"What's the matter?"

"I wouldn't mind a cup, but…"

"But?"

He shifted around on the step, embarrassed. "I'm afraid, you know, if things start to happen…I'm afraid I might pee in my pants."

Liz smiled, set a hand on his knee. "My medical opinion, my friend, is if things are happening that'll make you wet yourself, wetting yourself won't be your biggest worry."

She came out of the house carrying a mug of coffee for herself, tea for Adam. She handed him his mug and took her seat, again, next to him on the step.

"I found the tea."

"Thank you." He cupped his hands around the mug, held it under his chin to bask in the wisps of hot vapor. Still, he shivered. "Gets chilly at night."

I don't think it's all about the night chill. "Peeing on yourself is one thing. But if you shit yourself…" She was gratified at the chuckle that brought. "I remember reading that because of the adrenaline rush, some soldiers in combat even have erections."

"Oh, God, are you serious?"

"Medical fact. Speaking of medical facts, Adam…"

"What?"

She hesitated. It had been poking at her since Adam had decided back at Morahan's to make his stand, but at the same time… Hadn't she brought up enough ghosts from the poor man's past?

"No, go ahead," he pushed.

"Why are you doing this?"

He nodded. He understood the need for the question. "There's that woman, still laying out in that field because of me. Your friend, the constable…because of me."

She weighed that for a bit. *Not enough.* "Adam… Did you ever hear the phrase, 'suicide by cop'?"

"What's that?"

"Somebody wants to -- …" She couldn't get herself to say the words. "Well, they don't want to…to live. But they can't bring themselves to, um…"

She could see him mentally filling in the blanks. "Ok."

"So, they put themselves in a situation where the police do it for them."

"You think that's what I'm doing?"

"I don't know. That's why I'm asking."

Adam looked up at the night sky. She could see him sifting through it all, trying to be truthful to himself as well as to her. "If it makes you feel any better, I still don't want to die."

"I'm having trouble believing you're doing this over two people you didn't know. Oh, I believe you feel guilty about that. Still…"

"I can't run. Like you said: if they catch me on the road --"

"Bullshit. Why're you doing this?" She surprised herself at how bluntly it came out.

He took a moment. "I owe."

"Adam, you don't owe --"

"My wife and daughter. I have to make it worthwhile that I didn't follow them. Do you understand?"

And she did.

"You didn't have to stay," he said. "What's that about?"

She shook her head, grinning at her own confusion. "I'm not really sure."

"What do you think?"

"Alfie." And then it became as clear as those crystalline lights spread across the heavens. "You."

They leaned against each other, then, shoulder against shoulder, and sat like that for a while. For a moment, Liz could forget why they were there, the shotgun leaning against the steps nearby, and just be what they were: two people sitting on their front steps at night, watching and listening to a country night.

The Dark

Chapter Twelve

"What time is it?"

Liz was sorry he'd spoken, brought them back to where neither of them wanted to be. She didn't know how long they'd been sitting there, but her coffee, untouched in its mug, was cold. Tiredly, she looked to her wrist and then remembered that she hadn't bothered to put on her watch when Jocko Morahan had dragged her out of bed that morning. "I don't know. Feels late," she said through a yawn. "Does it matter?"

"I was wondering when they might get here."

"There's the travel time. And I imagine there'd be a goodly amount of discussion about what they're going to do, maybe some persuading will have to be done."

"Maybe they won't come."

Liz shook her head. She could tell Adam didn't believe it himself. "Parfitt will tell them that with the dead woman, they're committed. In for a penny..."

"Do you think they'll all come? Everybody that's on that list?"

"Just the ones he can trust to do what he wants them to do. The ones too scared not to come. We haven't talked about, well, have you thought about what you're going to do? I mean, do you have some kind of plan?"

Adam grinned. "You're asking a lot of somebody who just found out his name a couple of hours ago." Then his face went cold. "I want them – I need them -- to come after me; I don't want anybody else hurt."

"The rest of the town is dark; that shouldn't be hard."

"After that..." He looked down at the shotgun laying against the stairs by his side.

"It occurs to me that at some point someone's going to wonder if there's another way into this place."

"Is there?"

"There's a back door. It's in pretty bad shape; it won't take much for someone to force it. And you can't watch the front and back at the same time." She started to rise. "I think I can --"

He grabbed her hand. "Liz --"

She set her other hand over his. "I don't want to die, either, Adam."

He squeezed her hand once, she squeezed back, and then he let her go.

In her treatment room, Liz went to her supply cabinet and pulled out all her cartons of #5 surgical steel suture; the strongest she had on hand. She tied the end of one length to the handle of the lowest drawer at the foot of her exam table, then ran it across the room to the handle of another drawer at a work counter on the opposite wall, about shin high, allowing just enough space for the back door to swing clear. Knotting lengths together, she ran the suture back and forth several times for strength. She turned off all the room lights except for a few low lamps at some of the work counters along the walls. The room light would be dim enough that someone coming through the door wouldn't see the suture, particularly that far below their eyeline.

She went back to her bedroom to get the vial of pentothal, got herself a fresh syringe and drew 75 milligrams from the vial: the maximum safe dose. Then, thinking *Safe for who?*; she drew a few extra milligrams, figuring she'd fudge that part of the story if she ever had to explain her actions to the state licensing board. She set the syringe down on the exam table.

The suture should – she hoped – trip whoever came through the door, but that didn't mean they'd stay still long enough for her to hit them with the needle. Grimly accepting that this was going to have to be even uglier than she'd first thought, she went back to her bedroom and wheeled out her medical stool from where she'd left it by the bed and parked it by the exam table.

"I think this might be them!" Adam called from out front.

He was standing on the top step, the shotgun looking just as unwieldy in his hands as it always had. He pointed south, down the highway. Liz stood by him, saw the far-off glow of headlights.

"Probably. You better come inside."

They stood on either side of the open front door. Liz flicked on the office overhead lights; the only lit houselights in this part of Warsaw.

Now, from Carl's church, frantic guitar riffing of Angus Young, AC/DC chanting behind it: *THUNDER…THUNDER…THUNDER…*

And then Brian Johnson's shredded vocals –

I was caught

In the middle of a railroad track -- THUNDER

I looked 'round

And I knew there was no turning back – THUNDER

Out of that glow down the road came two cars. Liz recognized Parfitt's car in the lead, a dark SUV following.

"Do you believe this?" Adam said. "I'm shivering *and* I'm sweating!"

"Me, too." As the two vehicles drew close, Liz felt her knees start to go weak, a coldness in the pit of her stomach. *You can't be like this, lady! Not now!* She looked across at Adam, wiping at his damp forehead with his sleeve, still trying to find a comfortable way to hold the shotgun. *I need to be what he needs…or we're both dead.*

And then her knees no longer wavered. The fear in her gut was still there, but she'd dealt with that before, in the Boston General ER. It was a constant: terror someone on the table would bleed out faster than she could stitch a wound closed, frightened she couldn't get Narcan into an OD'd junkie before he went into arrest… Any number of times she'd faced, with fear, the prospect of someone dying in her hands…but had learned to keep working, keep making the necessary moves. *You can do this*, but the voice in her head wasn't hers. She almost laughed: it was Ellis's.

That was the trick, she thought grimly; she had to work this, think this through, coldly problem solve…like Ellis.

Parfitt's car and the SUV pulled up in front of Morohan's. Two men climbed out of each vehicle. One – she presumed it was Parfitt – stood at the front window, peering into the dark dining room. He tried the locked door.

"Are you ready?" Liz asked Adam quietly.

"No, but…" and managed a tight-shouldered shrug.

Liz flicked the front room lights on and off. One of the men poked Parfitt who turned, looked toward Liz's house. Liz turned the lights off. The four men climbed back into their cars, then pulled up on the road shoulder in front of her house. They got out of their vehicles, three of them lining up behind them, the fourth – the moonlight picked out Parfitt's cold face – taking a few steps toward her house.

"Adam!" Parfitt called out. "Adam! Or whatever the hell your name is! I'm guessing we wouldn't be here like this if you hadn't figured stuff out. Am I right?"

Liz looked over at Adam. His breathing was fast, she could see his face gleaming with sweat. It looked as if he were about to say something…then shook it off.

"Adam! Let's stop playing games! You know what I want! Just give me the list and we'll take off! Without the list, you've got no proof of anything, so wouldn't have any reason to get ugly. The woman, Dinsmore, I know, we all feel bad about that, but it wouldn't have happened if she hadn't been such a hardhead…like you're being right now!"

Hardhead. Liz remembered the photos from the woman's wallet; a young couple, everything ahead of them. She thought of the little trinket box, something saved from childhood. Hardhead.

"And, yeah, I get it, about the doc's friend, the cop or whatever he was. I'm sorry about that, I really am. It was a mistake, I'm sorry."

A mistake, and in Liz's head she saw the phone cord pulled so tight around Alfie Aubry's neck it was sunk into the flesh.

"But I can come up with a good story about what happened out here, believe me, and if we can all live with some stuff that went wrong, we can all walk away. But you decide to be some kind of half-assed hero, I guarantee you, you're not gonna see the sun come up tomorrow."

Parfitt waited for a response.

Liz looked to Adam again. His head was hanging down on his chest, moving slightly from side to side. *He doesn't know what to do.*

"Listen, my friend," Parfitt finally went on, "you better consider something; that this isn't just about you. You make a fuss and there's a good chance your doctor friend is gonna get hurt. Maybe more than hurt. I wonder if you've really thought about that."

Adam looked up at her.

"He's lying, Adam," she said. "He can't let us walk away. You know that."

"I know."

"What's it gonna be, Adam?" Parfitt called up to the house.

You've been…thunderstruck

Both barrels of the Purdey flared, Liz's front yard momentarily lit up, as if by lightning, the detonation echoing across the highway. She heard glass shatter. She peeked beyond the doorsill in time to see Parfitt take a running jump up onto the hood of his car and go skittering across to the shelter of the far side. The jagged edges of what was left of the SUV's driver's window twinkled in the moonlight.

Adam looked back to Liz, seeming almost apologetic. "I couldn't think of anything else to say."

"Reload, Adam. Reload!"

He cracked the breech, the empty shells went clattering across the office floor as he managed to fumble fresh shells into the shotgun.

Liz could hear voices outside:

"What the fuck, man! You said they didn't have guns!"

"This ain't how you said it was gonna be! You see what that sonofabitch did to my window? My wife's gonna kill me!"

"Fuck you, fuck your wife, sue me, I was wrong! You think this changes anything?" Then toward the house. "You wanna play that game, Adam What's-Your-Face? Then fuck you; you got it!"

The four men opened up with their pistols, rapid fire, peppering the front of the house. Liz went into a crouch, hemmed in by flying glass behind her as her windows imploded, splinters from around the doorsill in front of her. Then Adam was pulling at her, almost dragging her across the room to get behind the heavy wooden bulwark of her desk.

The firing let up. Liz guessed they were probably reloading.

"You happy now, asshole?" Parfitt called to them. "Change your mind about playing Alamo?"

"Help me with this," Adam said, and she grabbed the front edge of the desk alongside him, heaved until it went over on its side with a crash. Adam shimmied it into an angle with the desktop facing the open front door.

From outside, low murmurs by the cars.

They're working out a plan.

"I think it's time, Adam." She started to crawl for the hallway leading to the back of the house.

"Liz --"

"You just watch that front door."

He wanted to object, she could see it, but she could also see him accepting that as far as options went, there weren't any.

Liz scurried to her treatment room, crouched down in the shadows behind the exam table.

Firing started up again at the front of the house, but she could hear it was lighter, fewer guns, knew it was simply to keep Adam's head down while some of them made some kind of move.

She watched the rear door. *Any minute...Any second...*

Between the cheap lock and the weather-rotted wood of the doorsill, it only took one well-placed kick to pop the door free. A bulky figure in dark clothes came charging through the doorway, pistol stretched out in front of him, but in only two steps the suture caught him across the shins and down he went with a surprised yelp flat on his face.

Hope you broke your goddamned nose…

The room lit up for a flash and her ears rang with the thunderclap of the Purdey going off in the front room.

Liz didn't wait for the fallen man to recover. Even before he hit the ground, she was up, the stool in her hands, raised up, and while the gunman was still prone on the ground, Liz brought it down on his head. With the odd shape of the stool and rushing the blow, she hadn't caught him cleanly on the head, but it was enough to leave him momentarily stunned, and a moment was all she needed. She scooped up the syringe from the exam table and jumped on the man's back, flattening him against the floor with a breath-exploding *"Oof!"* She grabbed a handful of his hair with her left hand, pulling his head back to expose his neck. She made a best-guess in the dim light and plunged the needle into what she hoped was his jugular vein and jammed the plunger full down.

He screamed as soon as the needle bit, writhing while she held on, draining the needle into him, before he finally roused himself enough to buck her off like a crazed horse. She fell backward, watched in alarm as the man managed to struggle to his knees. Dark tendrils across his face from his smashed nose gleamed in the faint light.

Liz scrambled to her feet, grabbed the stool again, but the man had shaken off his daze, grabbed her right wrist with his free left hand and wrenched it so hard she howled in her own pain, dropping the stool. The man staggered to his feet, still holding her wrist then shoving it hard against her chest knocking her down to the floor, painfully landing on her rear.

"What did you do to me?" he screamed down at her. Then he saw who he was grappling with. "Bitch! Did you poison me? By Christ, I'll kill both you miserable shits myself!"

Liz started to crawl backwards away from him.

He took a step, but his legs seemed shaky, he shook his head trying to clear a growing fog. "Fuck you lady! If I'm going to hell, you're gonna beat me there!" He started to raise his pistol.

She recognized the blocky shape of the police Glock, could make out, even in the dim light, the dark, bottomless eye of the muzzle coming up slowly…up…

C'mon! she prayed to the saving god pentothal, *C'MON!*

Before the man could raise the pistol high enough to aim, it seemed as if his arm had suddenly been burdened by a great weight, he struggled to pull it higher…

"What the fu-..." he gasped, "Wha-...Wha'd you do..."

And then, like a felled tree, he fell straight over on his face.

She crawled over to him, felt his pulse, didn't feel particularly gratified to find it healthy, but she knew the shot she'd given him would keep him under for a good while. She groped around in the shadows, followed his right arm to the pistol, grabbed it in her left hand, and, cradling her painful right wrist against her chest, ran back to her office.

Adam was still behind the desk, his eyes wide and locked on the empty doorway, the shotgun aimed across the rim of the top. The room was filled with the acrid smoke of burnt powder. In the doorway, she could see two booted feet belonging to the body stretching down the length of the front stairs.

"I think...I think I killed him," he said weakly.

Liz took another look at those two unmoving feet. "This close, I'd be surprised if you didn't. Did you reload? Adam, did you reload?"

Adam shook off his fog, fumbled two fresh shells into the shotgun.

She held the Glock out to him. "Do you want this?"

"I don't even know what I'm doing with this thing," he said nodding at the shotgun. He saw the way she was babying her right wrist. "What happened?"

"I fell wrong, don't worry about it."

He nodded down the hallway behind them. "What about, uh…"

"Don't worry about him, he's out of the fight."

Adam looked back to the empty doorway. "What do you think they'll try next?"

"Med school classes didn't include combat tactics, so your guess is as good as mine. I guess we wait."

Liz wasn't sure how long they sat there in the shadows, hunkered down behind her desk, eye on the night-filled rectangle of her front doorway. She knew the time distortion effects of stress and adrenalin; they probably had only been crouched there, still and quiet, for only a few seconds but they felt minutes long.

After a while, she heard Adam let out a long, sighing breath. "I'm sorry I got you into this. I should've sent you out with Violet."

"You mean *order* me to leave? You could've tried."

Even in the dark, she could see his face wrinkle in a wry smile. Then his face went cold. "He's lost two men. He's not going to come in."

"We could wait him out, wait for Violet to send help."

He took a moment to weigh it, then shook his head. "I can't see him waiting. He's got to think we sent somebody out; he knows he can't sit out there forever. If he gets desperate, feels he has to make a move…"

Another shake of his head. "I told you; I don't want anyone else getting hurt."

"So…"

"So." He closed his eyes, his head bowed, Liz thought he almost looked like he was praying. Then his eyes opened, fixed on the open doorway in a hard, fixed way. "I don't want to, but I think I have to go out there. Don't look at me like that; I'm not crazy about the idea, either."

He waited, then; she could tell he was hoping she'd come up with a better, safer idea, but like Adam, she didn't see they had any other moves.

"Then I'm going with you."

"No," he said sharply, then laid a hand lightly on her knee, a kind of apology. "It's that I think it's better if you cover me from the door."

Which made sense. "Ok."

He pointed at the pistol in her left hand. "Can you hit anything with that?"

She hefted the pistol. It felt as awkward in her weak hand as the Purdey looked in Adam's hands.

"No, wait," he said, "I don't think I want to know. Look, um Liz…I mean everything you've done today…"

There was nothing else and Liz understood; they had reached a point where there were no words. The feelings were unsure: adrenaline, events of the day shared, heat of the present moment…she knew anything she was feeling just then could hardly be trusted, and the same went for Adam.

Yet…

She leaned in and kissed him, lightly, on the lips, lingered a bit. She felt his lips return the kiss; fingertips graze her cheek.

He withdrew slowly, let out something between a sad and satisfied sigh. "I guess we'll have to talk about this later."

"I guess."

"Are you ready, Butch?"

She shrugged. "You, Sundance?"

"No, but what the hell, right?"

They stood. Adam moved slowly toward the open door, the shotgun held out in front of him, while Liz stepped to the side, sheltered by the edge of the door frame. He motioned for her to take a place against the front wall, just to the side of the doorway.

Adam took a breath, a shudder seemed to go through him, then he began moving toward the doorway. He paused just short of the doorway, the muzzles of the shotgun's two barrels jutting out over the front stairs. She could see him trying to figure out how to step around the body there.

Someone must have been standing on the stairs just to the side of the door; they grabbed the barrels of the shotgun, yanking the gun so hard it pulled Adam's fingers against the double trigger and the Purdey fired off into the night. The same strong grip pulled the gun free of Adam's hands, then shoved it back against him, spearing his middle with the stock hard enough to punch the air out of him and knock him back against the floor. The gun was pulled away and flung it out into Liz's front yard.

It had all happened in an instant, leaving Liz frozen in surprise at first, but when she saw Adam go down, her instinct was to go to him even as she was trying to point the Glock at the open doorway where she knew a threat would appear. But the gun was awkward in her left hand and when she saw a figure in the doorway, the one shot she fired went wild, thudding into the wall. Before she could get a second shot off, the pistol was pulled from her hand and then…

Her head exploded in blinding pain as the pistol whipped across the right side of her face. The pain, the flash of white behind her eyes was so great she never felt herself fall to the floor, wasn't even aware she had until she forced herself into a fuzzy awareness, trying to focus through teary eyes. The man who had hit her was standing over her holding her pistol in his left hand, his own gun in his right leveled at her. "Jesus, lady, what'd you think you were gonna do with this?"

She couldn't see his face but recognized the voice: Parfitt.

Parfitt shook his head dismissively and threw her pistol out the doorway. He turned to Adam who was still struggling to get his breath, trying to get to his feet, to get to her.

"Liz…" he gasped.

Parfitt shook his head again, turned to Adam and delivered a hard kick to the right side of Adam's face sending him flat onto his back.

Liz wanted to crawl to him, but her own pain was too great, and now she could feel the warm crawl of blood down her face, down inside her collar.

"We didn't have to do this this way," Parfitt said, bending over the prostrate Adam, wagging a reprimanding finger. "But you wanted to be an asshole. You killed two of my guys, you prick, and now your girlfriend here is gonna pay for that, too. I warned you about this, my friend, but oh, no, you wouldn't listen! You just had to be an asshole!"

Parfitt stood, raised his pistol, aiming it at Adam's head.

Adam held up a hand, looking for a pause. "You kill me," he gasped, still unable to draw a full breath, "and you'll never find that list."

"Dumbass! *Dumbass!*" Parfitt chuckled. "I kill you and *nobody* finds the list and that works out just fine for me!" He shook his head: "Stupid," and he brought the pistol up again.

There was a thunderclap and lightning flash in the office that left Liz momentarily blind and stunned, that fueled the throbbing pain already in her head so hotly she thought her skull would explode. When her vision cleared, she saw Parfitt was lying face down on the floor. In the moonlight coming through her shattered windows, she could see the back of his jacket soaked with blood and looking like it had been run through a shredder. She wiped the tears out of her eyes. She couldn't see the face of the man standing in the doorway holding his smoking shotgun, but she instantly recognized the short, stout silhouette.

"Jocko!"

Morahan quickly reloaded his Purdey, kept the gun aimed at Parfitt though it was clear it wouldn't be needed. He stepped over to Liz. The look on his face gave her some idea of how bad the gash on her face must've been. "Oh, Jeez, Doc, look what he did to you!"

She held out her good arm for him to help her to her feet. "What the hell're you doing here?"

"I'm sittin' in my place, I could here all what's goin' on here, and I figured, well, I thought, you know, Doc Lizzie, that's my friend over there. How'm I gonna stay in my hole?"

She let herself fall against him in a hug, kissed him on his – as always – unshaven cheek.

"Look," Morahan said, "don't tell Vi what I did. She'd be real ticked off at me."

Despite all the pain in her head and arm, Liz had to laugh. "You're priceless, Jocko!" She shuffled over to Adam whose face didn't look much better than her own. "Are you ok?"

Adam managed a twisted little smile. "You're kidding, right?"

She and Morahan helped him to his feet.

Then Liz froze. "I forgot."

Adam was jumping to the same thought. "There's another one."

"Um, yeah," Morahan said, looking oddly uncomfortable. "He, um…"

"Jocko?" Liz nudged.

"Well, Carl, uh…"

"Jesus!" and on wobbly legs, Liz managed to stumble over the dead man in the doorway and stagger across her front yard toward the cars lined up on the shoulder. She could see Carl's burly silhouette outlined by the moon, stray hairs on his head catching the moonlight in a ragged halo. As she drew close, she could see Carl had something parked on his shoulder: a straight-edged shovel.

She came around the cars and saw Carl was standing over a figure prone on the ground.

"I don't know he's dead," Carl said. "Maybe, I don't know, I don't know, I only hit him the once, the one time."

Liz knelt by the figure, put a hand on his chest. Breathing was steady. The moonlight was enough to see that his face was a mask of blood, the nose smashed flat. She lightly probed the unconscious man's face, felt bones shift under her fingertips bringing a groan from the man, a wet gurgle in his throat. She was pretty sure most of the bones in his face had been broken.

"I was gonna hit him, again," Carl said, "You know, 'cause of Alfie, what they did to Alfie, I was gonna hit him, again, I really *really* wanted to hit him, again, I almost did, 'cause I, you know... But I didn't." His voice grew small, contrite. "I figured Alfie wouldn'ta liked that. What do you think, Doctor Lizzie?"

Liz stood. "I think Alfie'd be proud of you." She took him in her one good arm. "You're a good man, Carl," she said softly into his ear. "Anybody ever says different, *I'll* hit them with a shovel. Jocko, you and Carl help me get him inside. I've got to do something about his face before he chokes on his own blood."

"You sure you want to do that for this sonofabitch?" Morahan asked. "Pardon my language."

She looked over at Adam, and she felt he understood. "No," she said tiredly, "but, see, I took this goddamned oath..."

Lucidity

You've been…thunderstruck…

The Dawn

Epilog

They were all sitting at a table in Morahan's where they could watch the light show playing out against the early morning grayness: Liz and Adam, Morahan and Carl. Carl had set his sound system playing before he'd joined them. Jerry Garcia and The Grateful Dead:

Dawn is breaking everywhere, light a candle, curse the glare

Draw the curtains, I don't care 'cause it's alright

I will get by

Liz had managed to stitch up the gashes in hers and Adam's face, not too well since she'd had to do it leading with her left hand. "Like looking in a mirror," he said as she faced him while sewing him up.

"Yeah. A funhouse mirror."

Then he'd helped her get a brace on her wrist. She wasn't sure if Parfitt's goon had broken her wrist and wouldn't know for sure until she could get it X-rayed, but if it wasn't, he'd come close.

Morahan had poured them all snifters of his cheap brandy – "On the house" he said to everyone's surprise – although Carl had passed and was pulling on a long-necked Moosehead, explaining, "Suds is good enough for me."

The apron in front of Morahan's was filled with flashing lights. Amber from the work truck Community Phone had sent out to fix the phone lines. There were a lot of ambulance reds; Northern Light must've sent every rig they had, Liz thought, and still had to call on one of the local funeral homes because there were so many bodies to deal with. There was Alfie, of course, and they'd recovered the Dinsmore woman from the field, and there were Parfitt's two dead thugs. Then there was the one with the smashed face, courtesy of Carl, and the man Liz had put down who was still in his pentothal sleep and who'd no doubt be quite surprised when he woke up to find himself with a broken nose and handcuffed to a hospital bed with a state trooper standing over him. And then there were all those blue flashers on what seemed like every state police cruiser in that part of Maine.

"How do you feel?" Liz asked Adam as they sat there watching the bodies, living and dead, being carted out to their various rigs.

"Besides tired and hurting all over?"

"Besides that."

"I killed a man last night. I know I had to, but… I'm not sure I know how to feel about that."

"It may take a while," Liz said, and leaned against him, just a gentle bump of shoulder to shoulder.

I will get by

"I'm a little hungry," Adam said after a while. "I don't know if I can chew, but, Jocko, do you mind if I…?" and he nodded toward the racks of snack foods. Morahan, in more of his uncharacteristic largesse, signaled his approval with a wave of his snifter.

Adam roamed among the racks, sat back down next to Liz and handed her a package of Almond Joy. He held up his own: a package of Mounds.

Liz took the Almond Joy with a laugh. "Brandy and candy: breakfast of champions. I don't know if I can open this," and she held up her brace-encased hand. Adam did the honors.

A state trooper, who looked about fifteen with pimples to complete the picture, stuck his head in the door. "Mister Pratt? Lieutenant says we're supposed to escort you down to Augusta. Seems the state Attorney General wants to talk to you. You can follow in your car, or we can drive you."

"My car's --"

"We'll follow in my car," Liz jumped in. "They'll probably want a statement from me, too."

The trooper nodded. "We'll wait for you. Whenever you're ready." He started to leave…

"Hey, Trooper," Liz called and beckoned him over. She took the Dinsmore woman's little trinket box from the table and held it out to him along with her wallet and badge cover. "The dead policewoman; you should put this box with her personal effects. I think her husband's going to want it. Be careful with it."

The young trooper took the box as if someone had passed him a sacred relic and went back outside.

"Well," Adam said.

"Well," Liz said, and with pained groans, they both eased themselves to their feet.

Adam took Jocko's hand in both of his. "Jocko, I don't know how to, uh…" He shook his head, words failing.

Morahan shrugged. Liz knew; Morahan was thinking there was nothing to thank him for, he hadn't done anything any good Maine neighbor wouldn't have done. "Wanna thank me, when you get home, find your wallet and settle your tab. That'll be good enough."

Adam laughed. "Jocko, my friend, that hardly covers it, but you've got it!"

Then he turned to Carl. "What can I say, Carl?" He took Carl's hand in his. "Thank you doesn't seem to be enough."

Carl reached into his jacket pocket and came up with a crooked joint. "Gorilla Glue Number Four. For your head. You 'n' the doc might want to split that. I get to prescribe, too, Doctor Lizzie," he said, grinning at her.

Adam laughed and tucked the joint in his own jacket pocket. "Maybe later, Carl, but thanks. Again. For everything."

Liz gave Morahan and Carl a kiss on the cheek. "Thank Violet for me, Jocko – for us -- when she gets back. I don't know how long they're going to keep us in Augusta, so keep an eye on my place. My windows and doors are shot; make sure the racoons don't take up residence."

"We gotcha covered Doctor Lizzie," Carl said. "Right, Jocko?"

"Always," Morahan said.

"I know," Liz said. And then she found herself unable to move. She meant to turn for the door, tell Adam they should get going, but she could only stand there, looking at these two men who hadn't thought any more about risking their own lives on her behalf then if she'd come to them asking to borrow a cup of sugar. The pain in her head and arm fell away for a moment, she felt her chest swell, her eyes began to water.

"You better go," Jocko Morahan said quietly. "That junior cop is out there waitin' for you. We'll be here when you get back."

She couldn't stop herself; she grabbed them each in turn, hugged them hard, whispered a "Thank you," before she turned for the door, realizing for the first time – the very first time – since she'd moved to Warsaw…that this was home.

"You!" Morahan said harshly, pointing at Adam. "You make sure she comes back!"

Adam smiled. "I think we'll both be back," and he followed Liz out the door.

The Grateful Dead had finished and now it was Grand Funk Railroad. It was a song, Alfie had once told Liz, Carl used to play every chance he had when they were overseas.

If you return me to my home port
I will kiss you mother earth
Take me back now, take me back now
To the port of my birth

Morahan and Carl sat back down at the table. They watched Liz and Adam framed in the doorway, and as they crossed toward Liz's house to get her car, they saw them reach out to each other and their fingers intertwine.

"That's nice," Carl said. "I'll betcha, Jocko, I'll betcha inside a year, those two are married."

"Real bet?"

"Betcha twenny bucks cash money real bet."

"You're on," Morahan said, and they sealed the bet with brandy snifter clinking against beer bottle. "Bet you another twenty if that happens, they're divorced in two."

"You're on!" and they clinked glass again.

They sat there quiet for a while, then Morahan said, "Hey, Carl, ya know, I got this camp up on Moose Lake. What say we do some ice fishin' up there this winter?"

Carl's head lowered. "I was s'pose' to go ice fishin' with Alfie. We always used to go ice fishin', me 'n' him, me 'n' my friend Alfie."

"I know, Carl. That's why I'm askin'. You know; we both go up there for Alfie."

Carl turned to Morahan, he smiled sadly but warmly, and held out his bottle for another clink. "Yeah, for Alfie, yeah. You're a good man, Jocko," he said and drained the last of his beer.

"Don't let it get around. 'N' you want another beer, you're payin' for it."

I'm getting closer to my home…

Acknowledgments

A thousand thanks to Vijay Varu who gifted me his idea and let me grow it into this story.

Since I'm only a Maine transplant, if this story has any regional authenticity at all, that's to the credit of Amber Soha, my cultural guide to the area and who let me borrow from her own experiences growing up in rural Maine

About the Author

Aja lives on the coast of southern Maine where she teaches at a small university and loves to watch storms come in over the ocean. She shares her home with an adventurous shih-tzu and one judgmental cat. *Lucidity* is the second novel in her new series.